Lily

A Legacy of Hope

Learn more at www.thornberg.com

Thornberg Christian Books
Coolidge, Arizona 85128

Copyright © 2015 by Amanda Grace Hage
Copyright © 2015 by Gregory J. Thornberg

All rights reserved. No part of this publication may be reproduced, stored in a retrieval system, or transmitted in any form or by any other means including electronic scanning, photocopy, etc., except for brief quotations, as allowed by copyright laws, without the express written permission of the publisher.

ISBN-13: 978-1508560463
ISBN-10: 1508560463

Dedication

With all my love to my very special adopted
Grandpa Charlie and Grandma Jeanne.
And in adoration for my LORD
and my GOD,
who is the source of all
faith, hope, and love.

Chapter 1

"Can we go, Mama?" Jane danced on her toes in anticipation of her mother's answer. Just before everyone got up from their seats in church, Mr. Nelson had announced that Friday they were going to have a corn feed, and everyone was invited.

"I think so," Mrs. Wellington answered, chuckling softly at Jane's enthusiasm.

"Lily," Anna came over to her friend. "Mama's talking to your mama about you guys coming over on Thursday to help pick the corn. We're asking the Farns' and the Bryants, uhh…I mean Bartons, too."

"Oh, that would be so fun. I think we should be able to come—I hope we can."

Mr. and Mrs. Wellington accepted the invitation to help prepare and set up for the corn feed. Lily and her sisters happily anticipated the day, since they all loved harvesting.

"You're here!" Anna ran up to the wagon as Mr. Wellington stopped the horses at the Nelson farm Thursday morning.

"Luke and Danny will be here later to help with the tables and stuff. They wanted to get at least half a day of work in first," Lily told her as she jumped off of the end of the wagon. "Are the Farns' or the Bartons here yet?"

"No, but I expect they'll be here soon. Come on." Anna took off with Lily close behind and Jane and Olivia following. The girls ran to the back of the kitchen and picked up some burlap sack slings that had been made just for the purpose of corn picking. The towering corn plants soon swallowed the four girls. The noise of giggling and chattering voices accompanied the sound of snapping corn stems. It was not long before they returned to the house to empty their slings. Beth, Marylou, Claire and Alice Farns were in the kitchen with Susie, Emma and Marie Barton, preparing to husk.

"Alice, Claire, are you going to come?" Anna asked, as she and the other girls were about to leave again.

"No, we'll husk with the younger girls," Claire answered, selecting an ear.

"I'll husk, too," Susie volunteered.

"Oh, Susie, please come! It'll be so much fun," Emma begged. But Susie shook her head. Her younger sister sighed and went with the others.

The girls did have 'so much fun', which Susie later regretted missing. They chased each other down the long corn rows, raced to see who could move along and pick the fastest. Amidst their fun, the girls were still cautious and mindful of what their fathers always warned them about in corn fields...losing their sense of direction as well as each other among the tall stalks.

"How much more do you think we'll need?" Anna asked, when they made their second return.

"Oh, at least three or four more trips of this size," Mrs. Nelson answered, pulling off the silk. Gladly, they went back and made five more trips. The seven of them didn't realize how exhausting it was until they were all done.

"I'm bushed," Marylou dropped to the ground next to the enormous pile of husks.

"I'm not, I'm corned," Jane joked. The girls around her laughed.

"Luke," Mrs. Nelson said, when she saw him pass by. "Would you be so kind as to find Ed and tell him I need the big cast iron pot I use for laundry to be set up in the fire pit? Could you help him with it, too? It's really heavy."

"Sure thing."

"Thank you."

When the pot was ready, all of the women gathered the husked ears of corn and carried them to the pot.

"It's going to take forever for it to boil," Olivia commented, when she dumped her corn in.

"I know, we'll have to start it early in the morning. We'll be roasting some, too," Anna said.

When they had finished with the last of the preparations, Mr. Wellington stood from his reclined position on a fence post. "Well, I suppose we ought to get home and do our chores. Lil, will you go get the twins and Danny? I think they're all in the back pasture."

"Yes, Papa," Lily ran off in the direction she was told. When she reached the back pasture, she found Danny racing horses with the Nelson and Bryant boys. Jimmy and Johnny sat on the fence cheering with Frank and Eric Nelson and Ryan Farns. Sneaking up behind the fence, Lily put her arms around the twins and pulled them off it.

"Hey!" Jimmy yelled, as he felt himself falling with his sister's arms catching him.

"Wha'd ya do that for?" Johnny demanded.

"Papa says it's time to go." Lily smiled down at them.

Eric, Frank and Ryan gave a cheer.

"Who won?" both the boys were back at the fence in a flash.

"Now you made us miss it, Lil," Jimmy complained.

"Danny and Amber," Frank told them.

"Amber won?" Now Lily was interested. She followed the other boys to where their brothers were rubbing down the sweaty animals.

"It's time to leave, Danny," she repeated the message as she stroked Amber's velvet nose.

"Okay," Danny rubbed the horse's withers.

"How'd Amber win? She's never raced."

"I don't know, but I think I'll race her from now on—oh, but only if Your Highness permits," Danny bowed mockingly. The horse wasn't Lily's, but when Amber was first bought, she had arbitrarily claimed it. Now she couldn't live it down.

"Of course," Lily played up to his mockery.

"I don't think I've seen such speed since riding in the cavalry," William turned to Danny from rubbing his own horse down. "She's gotta have some thoroughbred in her."

"Probably, I don't exactly remember what Mr. Nelson said she is. Hey, Ed, do you remember what Amber is?"

"Let's see," Ed thought a minute, "as I recall, her mother was half quarter horse, half thoroughbred, and her father was half Arabian, no—maybe a quarter and something else, I can't remember. Maybe more quarter horse…I don't know. All the horses we've bred run together after a while—but yeah, she's got thoroughbred in her."

"I'll never forget when her pa threw me," said Dick. "Haven't forgotten to use my knees after that."

As they all walked back, Lily got bored with the racing talk and hurried ahead to see Anna and Beth a little bit more before they had to leave.

Olivia grabbed her older sister's hand the next day. "Come on, Lil, the three-legged race is going to start!"

"Coming…"

They tied their legs together and walked to the starting line. There were several other young people entering the race as well.

"Let's win this one, Liv. Start with the inside foot and then go outside. So inside, outside, inside, outside," Lily's competitive spirit showed. They had lost the gunnysack race and follow the leader as well. At Mr. Nelson's call they were off. It took a moment for the sisters to get used to the rhythm of it, but once they were, they went pretty fast.

"Come on, Liv, we have to beat Danny and Dick!" Lily gasped. Both of them screamed as they reached for the ribbon that marked the finish line. On the last step, Olivia's foot bent sideways and she stumbled bringing Lily down with her.

"We won, Liv! We won!" Lily looked back to see that the boys had fallen, too. Olivia was just as excited. Lily untied the ribbon, stood up and turned to help Olivia.

"Oww!" Olivia sat back down as soon as she tried to get up.

"Liv, what's wrong?" Lily knelt down again and Danny came over.

"My ankle got twisted. It's not too bad. I should be able to walk in a minute."

"Let me see, Livy," Danny got down and took off her shoe, and felt her ankle. "No, you should rest. It's pretty bad, 'cause it's starting to swell. Needs to get some ice on it."

"But—" Olivia wanted to protest, but she just sighed instead. A minute later, she was surprised when Danny picked her up and carried her to the shade of a nearby tree where she could see everything that went on. Olivia was somewhat embarrassed because by that time everyone had gathered to find out what had happened.

"Here, Livy, I brought you some ice and some company." Luke gave her Melly Jane. "Livia" was one of Melly's favorite aunts.

"Thanks, Luke," Olivia smiled.

The fun went on, and Olivia watched disappointedly from the background though members of her family often stopped and sat with her. But at least it didn't affect her appetite when it came time to eat the fresh hot buttered corn.

As darkness came, everyone sat around the fire that had cooked most of the corn and sang songs. But for Olivia's sake the Wellingtons did not stay long.

~~~

"Ready, Mama?" Luke asked, coming through door. "Lil and Liv are in the rig."

"Coming. Now you behave for Aunt Pearl," Mrs. Wellington turned to her remaining children. "We'll be back in plenty of time for supper. Thank you, Pearl…now take it easy, remember? Make them do the work."

"I'll be fine. Don't worry. It wasn't so very long ago that I lived here, in fact, it was barely a year ago," Pearl Glenn smiled at her sister-in-law. "We'll have lots of fun. You just go find a special ring for Alice." She followed Mrs. Wellington out the door.

"Well, girls, I think you know what Alice would like best. So what kind of ring do you suggest?" Luke asked, when the horses were well on their way.

"Nothing flashy…" Lily answered.

"But it should be elegant and pretty. Not plain or normal," Olivia added.

"What jewelry isn't pretty?" Lily teased, knowing what her sister meant.

"But it should not be extravagant in price," Mrs. Wellington put in the practical side. "Food, clothing, and other provisions are much more important. And you and I both know that she would much rather be provided for in that way than to have a fancy ring."

"Of course, Mama, but it should also show her how much she means to me…that I'll do anything for her, no matter how much it may cost."

"Hearing that makes me feel like I'm twenty, sitting by your father's side." Mrs. Wellington squeezed his arm. "That is almost exactly what he said when I asked why he bought me this ring when money could've been spent on more practical things. Now whenever I see it, I'm reminded of that and I thank God every day for his willingness to provide for his family."

"Well, he pretty much raised me, so I'm not surprised I sound like him. Pa sure is a special man," Luke smiled.

"Is he meeting us in Brockton?" Olivia asked.

"Yep, 'round noon he said."

Olivia and Lily were both dazzled by all of the jewels and precious metals they saw at the jeweler's shop in Brockton. They had never seen such beauty. Pretty much the only jewel they had seen was on their mother's finger. Both of them had browsed all of the displays in the glass cases before remembering why they were there. The middle-aged jeweler's mouth twitched with a smile at all of their exclamations over the dazzling gems.

Their business was just getting underway when the marshal joined them. The end result of their efforts was a moderately-sized gold band imbedded with one small red gem. Red was Alice's favorite color.

On the ride home, Lily and Olivia almost constantly talked about the items of jewelry that they liked best and their favorite gemstones. Mrs. Wellington and Luke just smiled.

A week later, Luke returned by himself to pick up the finished ring. Of course, the girls had to see it.

"It's just an old colored rock." Johnny shook his head at their excitement.

"Yeah, what's the big deal?" Jimmy agreed.

While doing chores later, Danny and Luke laughed over the way everyone had "oohed" and "aahed" at the ring.

"I guess gems, silver and gold do strange things to people. Makes them want to steal, kill—marry," Danny commented as he pitched some fresh hay into a stall. "Mama's diamond has always dazzled me. There's nothing like it when you put it in the sunlight—rainbows go everywhere."

"Yeah, I remember in school when I needed help I'd start playing with it on her finger while she was explaining something to me," Luke reminisced. He continued after a drawn out pause. "I've really been blessed, you know that? Thirteen and would've been sent to the Brockton Orphanage with no one in the world to care. Yet Pa and Mama were right there for me—with you and all the rest when my father and mother died. Sure they were friends, but they could've easily let me go. I'll never forget that day. The orphanage was staring me in the face and I hated it already. Then Pa and Mama came and told me I wasn't going. I think it was the best day of my life."

"I won't forget that day either. I thought I'd died and gone to heaven to have an older brother—it wasn't easy having three younger sisters." Danny put his pitch fork in its place. "Things'll be different again when you're married. I'm too used to having you around. But at least it'll be easier than last time you left, since this time you're staying in Oakville."

"I haven't even proposed to Alice yet," Luke objected, touched by his younger brother's openness of feeling.

"Doesn't matter. You don't have to. She lights up like a firefly every time you're around—even if you're not paying attention to her. She'll say yes before you can finish asking her."

"I couldn't ask for a better brother, Danny, you're really something special," Luke said as they walked together back to the house.

~~~

In the second week of September, little Lucy Joy Glenn made her grand entrance into the world. She wasn't even a day old when thirteen cousins visited and held her. She was passed around to everyone. Mark and Pearl radiated with pride and joy.

The following Sunday, the Farns' came over to the Wellington's for dinner and when dessert had been finished, Luke asked Alice to go for a walk with him outside. She readily agreed, but was surprised when none of their sisters followed along. When they were well outside, Claire, Beth, Marylou and the Wellington girls gathered and began talking excitedly.

Luke and Alice enjoyed the beautiful view from the top of the hill that overlooked the Wellington property.

As they stood, Luke took her hands in both of his. "I love you, Alice."

Surprise momentarily shone on Alice's face, but then it registered and she met his eyes with an even gaze.

"Will you give me the blessing of being my wife, and Melly Jane's mama?"

An openly loving smile lit Alice's face as she spoke, "I would love to."

Luke pulled the ring out of his pocket and slid it on her finger.

For a little longer they walked on, talking and planning for their future. When they returned to the house, there was an abundance of hugs and talking. It was so obvious that Luke and Alice loved each other. The wedding day was planned for December twelfth.

Melly Jane looked very confused when she was told that Alice was going to be her mama.

~~~

Jimmy and Johnny pulled out the ladder they used for picking apples. The apple trees in back of the garden were laden with bright red fruit. Some of the branches were so low even Davy, Mickey and Rachel could reach them.

The boys set up the ladder for the girls. They preferred to climb the limbs and toss the apples to someone on the ground. Peter was in his glory. Mrs. Wellington sat him and Melly Jane down on a blanket with plenty of apples to play with while she worked.

"Mama, do you think it was an apple that Eve ate?" Johnny queried, testing his mother's catching skill by tossing an apple to her.

"I don't know, Johnny," his mother caught the shiny red fruit. "God doesn't say what kind of fruit it was that Eve and Adam weren't supposed to eat. But it did grow on a tree. It might have been a pear, plum, or peach, or maybe a cherry or an orange. On the other hand, it might have been a fruit that was special and only that tree produced it."

"If we don't know what kind of fruit it was, then why do we sing that song about Eve eating the apple?" Jimmy wanted to know further.

"I'm not sure, Jimmy, that's a good question; come to think of it, the words don't make much sense. Whoever wrote it probably said it was an apple because they wanted to put a name to the fruit and apples are very common." Mrs. Wellington caught the next apple that was thrown her way just as a cry for help and the crashing of branches came from one of the other trees. Everyone rushed to see what had happened.

"Jane, are you all right?" Mrs. Wellington knelt down next to where her daughter lay flat on her back underneath the ladder, which Lily was quickly removing.

"I think so; nothing feels hurt. My breath is just knocked out of me." Jane propped herself up on her elbows.

"You sure?" Olivia double checked. "What'd you do?"

"Reached too far and lost my balance. I tried to regain it by grabbing the ladder, but I ended up bringing it down with me." Jane half smiled.

"Well, you rest a minute with Peter and Melly," Mrs. Wellington told her.

"Yes, Mama." Jane joined Melly and Peter, who were still enjoying the apples.

"Here, Livy," Lily called to her sister, holding her apron full of apples to be dumped. Accordingly, Olivia held up a bushel basket that was already partially filled. Lowering her apron, Lily let the fruit roll into the basket trying not to bruise them.

"We'll be doing nothing but canning tomorrow," said Olivia, putting the basket down.

"I know, but it's so much fun I don't mind."

"We won't, but our feet will. It's hot work, too."

The last bushel was picked in the early evening. Mr. Wellington and Danny arrived home just in time to help haul the heavy baskets to the porch to wait for processing the next day.

"I think I will be dreaming about apples for the next week," Olivia declared, getting into bed the next night. They had canned applesauce, apple butter, pie filling and just plain apple slices. What apples they did not preserve in jars were sliced and dried, or put in the cellar to use fresh over the next few weeks.

Olivia's prediction proved true. She even woke Lily up with her talking and arm movements that repeated what they had been doing all day.

~~~

Lily couldn't believe how fast the seasons changed. The leaves turned from their various shades of green to reds, oranges, yellows and browns. Several times she would stare out the window while assisting her mother with the others' schoolwork and see the colored leaves flutter down in the sunlight. They looked like colored confetti. Often, after the school books were closed for the day, the children would go out in the dry fallen leaves, raking up piles and jumping in them, as well as building houses with walls of piled up leaves.

The wedding preparations for Luke and Alice's wedding went smoothly as the fall deepened and slowly turned into winter. It was different for the Wellingtons to be the family of the groom, and not of the bride. On the wedding day, the ground was covered with snow. It was a pleasant sight to see the newlywed couple glide away in Luke's sleigh.

"Papa!" Melly Jane held out her little hand, opening and closing her fists repeatedly. "They'll be back in a few days," Lily soothed, picking her up. "You'll get to stay with Grandma and Grandpa 'til then."

"G'ampa?" Melly looked curiously at her aunt.

"Mm-hm," Lily nodded.

Luke and Alice returned from their week long honeymoon just in time to prepare for their first Christmas together as a family.

On Christmas Eve, the three branches of the Wellington household gathered together at the marshal's home.

"I can't remember the last time we spent Christmas with more family than just us," Mr. Wellington told his wife. "It's been years."

"It's wonderful, though—a bit crowded—but wonderful." Mrs. Wellington smiled as she watched Melly Jane run up to her great grandpa, Charles MacCrery.

"G'ampa! G'ampa, wook!" she said, holding out the dolly she had received earlier that day.

"Well, would ye look a' tha'. Ye're a real grown up girl wi' a bairn o' yer own now." Her great grandfather picked her up as she displayed to him the cherished gift. "What'd ye name yer wee one?"

"Baby." Melly hugged the soft toy.

"Ahh…should we read yer bairn a story then, so she can sleep? Maybe sing her a song, too?"

Melly Jane nodded. "I get da book," she said, sliding from his arms to retrieve the story she wanted.

The day was wonderful—many fond memories were made. They enjoyed part of the day outside sledding and skating. In the late evening, after supper and dessert were over, they sat around the fire singing carols and popping corn.

Chapter 2

"...Lord, please bless this new member of our family. Nurture it and knit it together with Your perfection. Please help Mama and give her strength, too. Give us all a good rest tonight, in Jesus' name, amen," Mr. Wellington prayed one night in the middle of January, after they'd had their family Bible reading.

Lily looked up from her mother to her father in astonishment. So were her other siblings.

"You mean...?" Olivia's tongue was the first to loosen.

"Mm-hm," Mrs. Wellington smiled. Her affirmation was followed by cries of delight as her eleven other children gathered around her.

Lily found herself impatient. She always did in the first days of her mother's pregnancies. Nine months always seemed an eternity to wait for a new baby.

~~~

"It's too hard," Sarah complained. She and Lily were sitting at the piano for their weekly piano lesson. Lily was not as excited about teaching piano as she had been the very first months when she had started a year before. She did not mind it, but it had taken on the feel of "another thing to do."

"It is not too hard," Lily tried to be patient and encouraging. "You can do it. God gave you a very good brain and made you very capable."

"I don't like it. It's too hard to watch the music and play the right notes. I need to see my fingers," Sarah persisted. She had turned out to be the most difficult of Lily's piano students.

"That's why you keep your fingers on the keys—so they don't move around and you have to keep track of where they are and where they should be," Lily explained again, for what felt like the hundredth time.

"That's why I keep my wrists down so they stay in the same spot."

"But that's bad posture. You can't play well that way. Now I want you to try this song again. The right way."

Sarah replayed the piece. Her lack of effort was obvious.

"Sarah, did you try your best?"

Silence.

"Sarah?"

Slowly, Sarah shook her head.

"You are able to do it. I've seen you. You've really tried before—why won't you try your best now?"

No answer.

Lily sighed. "Go tell Jane it's her turn," she nodded her head, motioning for her younger sister to go.

"Mama, she just doesn't have enough gumption. She doesn't try her best. I don't know what to do," Lily explained to her mother later.

"We'll just have to keep working on her. I'll have Papa talk to her," Mrs. Wellington responded.

"We're not as good of friends as we could or should be...and I think that's part of it. She just gets so antagonized when I try to tell her how to do something or what to do. I try not to be bossy. But there are times when I need to tell her what to do and correct her—especially with piano. It's like what we went through with her not listening about sweeping thoroughly a few weeks ago."

"I've noticed. I think I need to look up some verses from Proverbs about work like I did for you." Mrs. Wellington smiled with good natured teasing. But it was true. When Lily had been eight like Sarah, and a little older, she had hated kitchen work and every other chore. But God had changed that.

That evening, after her father's scolding and memory verse assignment, Sarah exited her parents' bedroom with a scowl. When she passed Lily, she gave her older sister a withering look.

Lord, help us to get along and love each other, Lily sighed in her mind. Eventually, Sarah's attitude improved, and so did her piano playing.

~~~

Ben sighed. Ever since George Hanson had announced what they were going to do to the marshal, he had not been able to sleep. It had been days. When his body would finally succumb, out of sheer exhaustion, he would wake up sweating and gasping from the most horrible nightmares he could ever imagine. They all seemed to have the same theme. He was standing in a ring of fire and a judge was looking down at him condemning him for his crimes, and sentencing him to eternal suffering in a fiery furnace. The one crime that was repeated over and over was the massacre of the Wellington family.

"I can't go through with it," he told himself. "I can't."

"What's with ya, Ben?" Jack asked, sitting down with his plate of beans. "Ya won't eat and ya got bags under your eyes."

"Ain't been gettin' good sleep," was all Ben replied.

"Don't worry, when we have Wellington gone you'll rest easy," Hanson told him. Ben winced, almost groaning at the thought.

"I'm leaving, George," Ben approached his boss later when everyone else was asleep.

"What? Where?"

"Don't know, but I can't stay 'round no longer."

"Why?" Hanson demanded.

"I can't live like this anymore. I've been havin' nightmares. Even you would be scared out o' your skin if you'd seen what I seen."

"What? Are you gettin' soft? Mush-headed?"

"You know me. I ain't never been mush-headed in my life."

"I don't know, you've been actin' strange lately. No, you can't go 'til after we're through with Wellington."

"But—"

"Don't you try, either—or else."

Ben nodded and left. He knew what Hanson's 'or else' was. It was something he didn't want to face on top of the dreams.

~~~

A bloodcurdling scream came from upstairs. Mr. Wellington jumped from his seat at the kitchen table where he was working figures with their expenses. Mrs. Wellington dropped her knitting needles. Forgetting their tasks, they rushed up the steps. Lily was calling them when they reached the top.

"What is it?" Mr. Wellington gasped, looking at his five horror-filled daughters.

"I opened the curtain to let the moonlight in and a man was looking in," Olivia trembled.

Mr. Wellington crossed the room to the window and opened it. No one was on the roof below the window. Shattering glass caused him to bring his head back inside.

"What in the world?" he walked out of the room.

"Pa!" Danny's voice resounded from the stairs as he descended them. "Fire!"

Mr. Wellington was there in an instant. Flames circled the perimeter of the kitchen, heavily blocking the front and back doors. The marshal did not need to wonder at it. He took the pot of leftover coffee and poured it in a line at the doorway of the parlor where the fire was rapidly heading. He wondered how much it would do. Danny soaked a towel and started beating the flames, as his father filled the pot with water and tossed it on the growing blaze. A moment later a gunshot shattered the kitchen window.

"Danny, go get the rifles now!" Mr. Wellington ordered.

Danny thought his life had ended when he entered his parents' room to find Ben there. In a flash he reached for his father's gun case.

"Wait," Ben grabbed his arm. Danny expected to be shot. "I'm here to help. You saved my brother's life," Ben continued, "and I saved your life once. Trust me. My debt ain't fully paid."

To Danny's frantic mind the outlaw seemed to be talking in riddles. But for some reason he yielded all the same.

"You go down to your pa. Try and keep the flames down, and put them out—they'll be closing in about now. I'll see to the rest of your family," Ben instructed, as they loaded the firearms. At his last words, Danny hesitated to comply.

"Trust me. I've been havin' hell fire dreams because of waiting for this night and if I don't help you, I will die with you." Ben's words were tense with emphasis and emotion. Danny finally nodded, though in his mind he didn't know why.

"They're circling the house now, Papa." Danny ran down the stairs. The flames had been gradually gaining on his father.

Mr. Wellington seemed to know it was Hanson and that the outlaw was closing in even before Danny had said it. "We've got to get your mother and brothers and sisters out."

"They are."

"They are? What?"

"God sent somebody and he's taking care of them. They're okay."

As Danny and Mr. Wellington kept the flames from spreading and exchanged gunfire, Ben took bed sheets and tied them together into a long, makeshift rope. Mrs. Wellington and the children assisted him, all the while wondering at the stranger who had suddenly appeared.

"We have to go out the back," Ben told them, when the last sheet was tied. He did not tell them that all sides of the house were covered and Hanson had ordered his men to capture any member of the family. But the back of the house was safer and Hanson was in the front. Quietly, Ben opened the window in the boys' room. Resting his chin on the sill, Ben cast his voice to the side of the house.

"Hey, guys! The boss needs us up front," he called. Lily's eyes widened as she saw three men appear from behind an apple tree, the large oak and one of her mother's bushes, and slink to the front of the house.

"Okay, we gotta hurry," Ben sent one end of the sheet rope out the window. "I think you should go first, Ma'am."

Mrs. Wellington took a breath, put her feet out the window and shimmied down. Jane followed her with Jimmy and Johnny. Next, Lily and Olivia harnessed Peter, Mickey and Rachel one at a time to the end of the rope. Then Davy and Sarah went and lastly Olivia and Lily.

"Run for the woods beyond the barn, they won't see you if you hurry. Carry the little ones," Ben instructed Lily as he let her down.

Lily's heart raced as she slid down the rope. The girls and their mother carried the younger ones. It seemed a long way until they reached the cover of the trees. When they were deep enough, they stopped. But Mrs. Wellington was worried. It was a cold February night. They had rushed out in woolen socks, flannel night shirts and shawls, nothing else.

"Come children, it's not that long of a walk to the Barton's. Your papa needs help and you have to stay warm," she decided briskly.

By the time the house came into sight, everyone's fingers and toes were numb. Rachel Wellington stumbled up the Barton's front steps. Her feet were barely working. Dr. Barton answered her loud knock.

"Rachel!" he exclaimed, looking beyond her to see the children following her.

"Tom, the house is on fire and Michael and Danny are still there. Hanson did it."

"Come inside," the doctor ordered, letting them all file in. Ellen Barton was no less shocked than her husband to see her best friend.

"Stephen," Dr. Barton turned to his sons, who were coming downstairs guns in hand in answer to his call. "I need you to ride and get Mark Glenn."

"I'm going."

When the men had left, Lily and Olivia relaxed more. They were both mortified to be seen in their nightgowns. Mrs. Barton bustled about warming cocoa and getting blankets and pillows to help everyone warm up.

"Now, Ellen, don't fuss, we're fine," Mrs. Wellington insisted. But seeing she wasn't heeded, she did all she could to help. The younger girls were excited about the "sleepover." When the edge of frostbite and numbness had been taken away, everybody settled down and got cozy. Mrs. Barton and Mrs. Wellington talked quietly in the kitchen over their steaming cups of cocoa. The boys bedded down and attempted to sleep. Olivia laid down with the younger girls, who were quietly whispering, and Lily sat on the cold window seat staring blankly down the road hoping for some sign of her brother and father. Scenes of what had happened flashed before her eyes. The startling face she and Olivia had seen in the window. The sound of crashing glass and crackling flames.

The choking stench of smoke. A stranger appearing out of nowhere, scaring she and her mother half to death. Villains coming from the shadows of the night and running away—and gunshots.

Oh, God, please save them—let them live. Protect them. The house doesn't matter—just bring Danny and Papa home safely. She prayed in agony at the thought of never seeing them again. Leaning against the cold window pane gave her a headache. But not wanting to leave the moonlit view, Lily took a pillow and put it between her head and the glass. Amidst her anxiety, she slowly fell asleep.

~~~

"No, Papa!" Danny pulled the barrel of Mr. Wellington's gun down. Ben had just come downstairs from ensuring that Mrs. Wellington and the children had escaped safely. "He took care of Mama and the others," Danny continued.

"I'm paying a debt, Marshal. I couldn't live with myself if I didn't help," Ben tried to explain.

Another bullet came whistling through the window.

"Danny, go upstairs and see if you can pick any of them off!" Mr. Wellington commanded.

"Yes, sir." Danny took the steps three by three.

"Grab a towel, Ben," the marshal turned to the man that was still with him. The sorrowful outlaw did as he was told. Subduing the fire as well as defending themselves was grueling work. Sweat crawled down their faces and necks. After a while, Mr. Wellington switched places with Ben.

"Mama musta got help, Pa! There are two guys coming down the road," Danny called from an upstairs bedroom.

Will and Dr. Barton turned the tables on Hanson and his gang. George was enraged. Why was his "fool-proof" plan failing?

"Okay, Wellington, your time has come!" Hanson ran to the back door and opened it with his loaded rifle ready. But the sight that met his eyes surprised him so much that he paused his attack.

The short moment that Hanson hesitated gave Ben just enough time to use his own firearm. Only one thing was on his mind. The dreams. The dreams that he seemed to be living didn't allow him to think about what he was doing. He just did it. George Hanson fell back in the snow. In agony, Ben leapt through the narrow boarder of fire and knelt by his side. The marshal was right behind him.

"Why?" Hanson gasped. "Why?" he angrily spewed.

"I got tired of following your low down ways; I couldn't live with myself if I didn't stop you, George. You never listened to me. I tried to tell you, but you never listened..." Ben gripped his brother's arm.

"Traitor," with the last of his strength Hanson jerked his hand away. A moment later, he died.

"George...!" Ben tried to get him to answer, refusing to believe that he was dead.

"Ben," the marshal called, bringing Ben's attention back to the flames which were growing rapidly again.

"Grab a bucket and get some snow!"

Even with a hurting heart, Ben did not delay in carrying out the command. Danny came downstairs to help, as he was of no use in the upper level. With access to snow and three of them, the fire began to shrink. Dr. Barton and Will, with the assistance of Stephen and Mark Glenn when they arrived, managed to capture the remaining men of Hanson's group.

When the last glowing embers had been extinguished, and everything soaked to ensure no recurring flames, Mr. Wellington, Ben and Danny walked through the charred front door.

"Are you all right, Mike?" Dr. Barton asked.

"Yeah, just scorched, where are Rachel and the children?" Mr. Wellington voiced the worst of his worries.

"They're at our place. They're fine."

"Thank You, Lord—Danny, will you go get the sleigh?" the marshal's mind returned to his present duty. "And some rope, too," he added to Danny's back. When Danny returned, the remaining nine outlaws were bound and put into the wagon. Ben went to the back of the house and bore Hanson's corpse back, laying it in the wagon bed. Salty tears mingled with his sweat as he did so. He was thankful that it was too dark for anyone to notice.

"I'm sorry, Ben. I'll see what I can do in the morning," the marshal felt horrible tying the hands of the man who had done so much to help. But he didn't know what else he could do, or how far he could trust him.

"Will, Stephen and I can take them into town, Mike," Mark Glenn told Mr. Wellington. "You'll get sick if you stay out here any longer."

"Thanks, Mark," the marshal did not refuse the reins handed him. His jaw was beginning to chatter slightly. Danny fought to keep his own teeth still as he mounted behind his father.

Lily jerked from her light sleep at the sound of hoof beats. The others were sound asleep. From her perch on the window seat, she saw three men on horseback. Two of them she immediately recognized.

"Mama!" she whispered loudly, while getting up.

Mrs. Wellington roused from her slumped position on the kitchen table. "What?"

"They're back with Papa and Danny!"

Immediately, Mrs. Wellington was on her feet and at the door. Despite her bare feet, she dashed out onto the snowy ground.

"Are you all right?" were the first words out of Rachel Wellington's mouth and she embraced her husband. Mr. Wellington nodded, still holding her tightly.

After hugging Danny, she walked with them to the house where Lily was waiting at the door.

"Did you get Hanson and his men?" Lily asked, when they had sat down at the table.

"Mm-hm," Danny nodded.

"What happened to the house?" Mrs. Wellington asked hesitantly.

"It's still standing. The kitchen needs a lot of work, part of the wall by the stairs is burned, and the doorways are charred as bad as the kitchen, but the fire didn't make it into the sitting room. So it's just the kitchen. I think we'll have to rebuild the whole room, though." Mr. Wellington rubbed his face with one blacken hand. Then he seemed to realize how dirty he was.

"I think we should wash up—come on, Danny," he went to the sink.

"You'd best go to sleep," Mrs. Wellington told Lily. Lily nodded, curled up on the window seat, admiring the moonlit snow 'til a peaceful sleep over came her.

~~~

Ben Hanson removed his boots and stretched out on the bottom bed of the bunk he shared with Jack Thomas. In the very depths of his soul he was mourning. His older brother lay dead in the snow at the back of the jail. Memories flashed through his mind. Scenes of him and George playing "Sheriff and the Bad Guy," doing chores together, going to school…the memories did not stop. But he constantly went back to their favorite game.

They always fought over who got to be the sheriff. Neither one of them had ever liked being the bad guy.

So why did we turn out to be the bad guys? he wondered.

The answer came in memories of their teenage years and young manhood. Sloughing off on chores, bullying their way to the top at school, disrespect for authority, carelessness in their responsibilities...it was a slow degrade from laziness to lust for money. Ben had followed his older brother, admiring him and wanting to be like him. But in years past, after the gang had been formed, Ben had left off being one of the leaders. He had found that he didn't have the taste for thieving as he'd had at first. He longed for his brother to stop, but didn't have the courage to stand up to him and leave. A small faint desire for a clean conscience and what was right had grown to an intense longing. It was a longing he had no idea how to quench. It had intensified with each misdeed. It grew stronger now with each thought. The night that Ben thought he would sleep peacefully was once again filled with the agony of fire and condemnation. Added to it now was the sorrow over the death of his brother.

Chapter 3

In the morning, the Wellingtons returned to the house to observe the damage in the light. After Mr. Wellington had made sure the stairs were sufficiently sturdy, the girls cautiously climbed up to get dressed. The boys were slower in following their mother's orders.

The house was in worse shape in the broad daylight than it had appeared in the soft moonbeams.

"What are we going to do, Michael?" Mrs. Wellington asked, wrapping her arm around his left one, as they stood together after examining the whole kitchen.

"Well...the repairs are so major that we can't live here for the time being...I'm thinking that we're going to have to rebuild this whole side of the house, from the stairs on. Good thing we built it geometrically, 'cause we'll have to rebuild our room upstairs, too. I don't trust those boards when their connections at the wall have been seriously burned. The rest of the house is sound and safe, though. The fire never touched it." Mr. Wellington looked around him, surveying more than just the burnt walls, ceiling and floor. "Tell the children to get their clothes and necessities packed. I think we'll go in town to the boarding house. Stay out of our room. I'll get the things in there."

Mrs. Wellington went to start gathering things together.

"Watcha thinkin', Pa?" Danny came next to him.

"I'm thinkin' God's going to keep Will and Stephen well supplied with work for the next four to six months…" the marshal grinned in spite of the fact that he had no idea how they would afford to pay for it.

~~~

Pictures flashed in the memory of Luke Wells, when he was told of the fire by Mr. Wellington.

"Are you all right, Luke?"

"Yeah," Luke shook himself. "I was just…" his voice trailed off, he couldn't say more since his throat was tight. The marshal put his arm around his son. He remembered. He knew and understood the pain Luke had in losing his birth parents in a fire.

"We're going to be staying at Mrs. Ellis's Boarding House."

"Mrs. Ellis's Boarding House?" Luke repeated. "No, Pa. You come and live with us 'til the house is redone."

Mr. Wellington shook his head. "No, Luke, having thirteen people invade Alice would be the worst thing for a new wife and mother."

"Not Alice. She wouldn't mind. Bring everybody for supper tonight and we'll see."

"Okay."

It was a hard day for the marshal. He had to contact Judge Frank Arnon in Charleston for help with legal issues.

"Marshal?" a voice came from the back prison cells, after Mr. Wellington had wrapped things up for the day and was about to leave. He turned and went to see who wanted him. It was Ben.

"I know I don't deserve no right to be asking favors—let alone getting them granted. But I need to ask, I gotta know…How do I get peace? I can't put all this to rest…how do I get a clear conscience? I keep having horrible dreams about dying."

Mr. Wellington shouldn't have been shocked after the past night's events. But he was. Standing in front of the iron bars, he was completely taken aback by the outlaw's hopeless plea for answers. Without a word, he turned and walked back to the front room. Ben's head hung in despair. It soon lifted with surprise at the sound of the marshal's returning footsteps.

"This holds all of the answers, Ben," Mr. Wellington held out the Bible that he always kept in his desk. "Read this part. It's the book of John. Read anything and everything else in it, too." As he spoke, he opened the Bible to the place he mentioned and gave it to Ben through the iron bars.

Ben took the book.

"Just read it, and believe it with all your soul." The marshal reached an arm through the bars and shook Ben's hand. "I'll see you tomorrow." He turned and walked away.

Deaf to the taunts and jibes that his fellow prisoners tossed him after the marshal had left, Ben Hanson slowly sat down on his bed. With excited fingers, he held the Bible and began to read thirstily. His parched soul eagerly drank in every drop of the Living Water.

~~~

Everyone was excited when Mr. Wellington arrived at the boarding house and told them of going to have supper with Luke and Alice. Jimmy and Johnny rushed out to the sleigh. They were already tired of the small room, after only four hours.

"Hello, come on in!" Alice cheerfully beckoned them when the sleigh slid to a stop.

"Luke home yet?" Mr. Wellington asked as they climbed the porch steps.

"Mm-hm, he's in the barn doing chores. He should be done soon."

As Mrs. Wellington and the children took off their coats and shoes, Danny and Mr. Wellington went to the barn to help.

"How bad was it?" Alice asked, when they were all seated in the living room.

"Bad...in fact, I'm not sure any of us would have survived without Ben. The kitchen is all burned. We're going to have to rebuild the entire thing. Michael says that we'll have to do our room and the stairs as well. He doesn't trust that part of the upstairs floor. The fire got to some of it."

"Who is Ben?"

"That's probably the biggest miracle of it all. He was one of George Hanson's men. Danny says Ben told him that they were brothers. Anyway, for some reason, he turned on his brother and helped the children and I escape, then did all he could to save Michael and Danny. Unfortunately, it came down to having to shoot his own brother."

"Oh, my! Well, considering all that's happened, I think you should stay here and not at the boarding house."

"No, that's out of the question. That'd be way too much stress for you. It wouldn't be right," Mrs. Wellington refused.

"Rachel, Luke would love it and so would I. We want you to stay. Luke built this house with plenty of rooms for the large family we hope to have some day—but since we don't have one yet, who would better fill those rooms than part of our family until your house is fixed?" Alice persisted.

Mrs. Wellington didn't respond. Alice was too sincere a girl to say something she didn't mean with all of her heart, but Rachel Wellington was still not totally persuaded.

"This is really good, Alice," Danny complimented his sister-in-law at the supper table.

"Thank you, I'm glad you like it. Hope there's enough for everybody. Will you pass me the potatoes please, Grandpa?" asked Alice, with a look at Luke.

"What?" Mr. Wellington picked up the dish and passed it with a puzzled expression. Then he saw his wife's face. Mrs. Wellington understood.

"Feeling old, Grandpa of *two*?" she laughed.

Mr. Wellington caught on. "Uh huh—Grandma," he responded.

"Is it really true, Alice? Is Melly Jane really going to be a big sister?" Lily asked.

Alice happily nodded.

"Now how about staying with us?" Luke persisted.

Mr. Wellington started to shake his head.

"Oh, please," Alice pleaded gently. "It would be no stress at all. It would be so wonderful."

"It would save money," Luke added, knowing it to be a weight on Mr. Wellington's mind.

"Maybe, but I would rather be scraping pennies the rest of my life than have a ruined relationship with my son and daughter-in-law. It's not worth it to me. I don't feel right about imposing my family on my son's. Suddenly adding thirteen more people when you're just starting out is…"

"Pa, have I ever lied to you about how I feel? Has Alice?"

Mr. Wellington shook his head. The argument against him was getting stronger.

"We really and truly want you to stay."

"All right," he consented. "We'll stay—but even if we become the least bit of a bother, then out we go."

All the children, who had sat silently listening and hoping, let out a loud cheer. Their enthusiasm made Luke and Alice laugh with pleasure that it was a unanimous agreement.

~~~

Judge Arnon was sitting at the marshal's desk the next afternoon when Mr. Wellington arrived.

"Hello, Frank. I didn't expect to see you here 'til tomorrow—how are you?" The marshal took off his hat.

"Fine, thanks, Michael. A lady came and asked Mark to check something out; he should be back soon. When I got your telegram saying you had Hanson's gang, I didn't lose any time. Just dropped everything and caught the next train. I brought the reward money, too. I've been waiting for years to get those guys to prison. How'd you catch 'em?"

"Well, it was more like they caught us. Set fire to the house. Only the kitchen was burned, but they would've had us for sure if it weren't for Ben."

"Ben? You don't mean Ben, Hanson's sidekick…turned on his boss? Hanson must be boiling. How are you keeping him quiet back there in the cells? If I remember right, he makes quite a ruckus."

"Hanson's dead, Frank—Ben shot him. Ben is Hanson's brother." Mr. Wellington nodded with his last words, attentively watching his comrade's expression change. "There is another reason to believe in God—besides the other million, Frank. You and I both know that Ben's heart was as cold and hard as stone…speaking of which, I have to go see him for a minute. Oh, and while you're getting out your papers, pull out a pardon slip." The marshal took the keys from his desk and strode to the back jail cells.

"How are ya, Ben?" he stopped at the last cell. Ben Hanson looked up. The Bible lay open on his lap.

"Marshal, I've never known this feeling in my whole entire life." His voice was awed. "I've never really had such peace or joy. I can't thank you enough."

"I can't tell you how glad I am, Ben. But don't thank me, I didn't save you and I didn't make you believe."

"But you told me. You obeyed what He said to do."

Mr. Wellington was amazed at how much Ben must have read.

"Enough of this religious jawin'. The judge here?" Jack impatiently questioned.

"Yeah, we'll be doing the others first, though. See you later." The marshal pulled out the keys from his pocket and opened the door of Rex and Mitch's compartment. They quietly followed him.

With a sigh, Frank Arnon asked the question for the ninth and final time, "How do you plea?"

"Guilty and forgiven," Ben answered straight out. Arnon looked at the marshal, who evenly returned his gaze with a silent "see what I mean."

"I'm not sure..." the Judge hesitated. There was a small nudge on his leg under the desk. With a reluctant look at Mr. Wellington and an expression of "I don't want to do this," he sighed: "By the power vested in me by the government of West Virginia—you are pardoned, Ben Hanson. You're a free man."

Ben barely got three words out, "Thank you, sir." He forced himself to go on. "Your Honor, if you don't mind, can I keep that paper that says I'm pardoned and go with the others to the State Prison?"

"Uhh...well..." Frank looked at the marshal, who gave just a slight nod. Completely confused and unsure, the judge consented.

"Marshal," Ben turned to Mr. Wellington. "I'm beholdin'. I know what I woulda gotten. I was ready and God's will be done—but there is so much I need to do. Would you mind if I keep the Bible?"

"It's all yours, Ben." Mr. Wellington turned to the guard that was with the other outlaws. "That's it, Jim."

"Okay, move out!" Jim prodded his charges. After shaking the hands of the marshal and judge, Ben followed them.

"What're you comin' for? You're the lucky one that's been pardoned," Jim asked the question all the outlaws wanted the answer to.

"I know, and now I have a job to do: telling others about God's pardoning grace." Ben jumped in next to Jack Thomas. Jim shook his head and locked the door securely.

"That's a strange one, Bill," he commented to his partner as the wagon jerked forward.

"You can say that again," Bill agreed.

~~~

"I don't know what I let you talk me into, Michael," Judge Arnon shook his head as he gathered his papers into his briefcase. "If and when he turns out to be the tyrant you claim he isn't, it'll cost you your badge—and me my profession, if not worse for the both of us. That man should've had the noose ten times over."

"If you only knew," the marshal put his hands in his pockets and relaxed in a chair.

"If I only knew what?"

"Frank, that man turned himself in of his own volition. He threw himself on my mercy. He saved my whole family. If it weren't for him, we'd be laying in our graves. On top of that, he shoots his own brother to save my life as well as my son's. Now, as a saved, born again believer, he goes to the prison he was freed from to tell others that are just like he was about God's salvation. Look me in the eye and tell me that Ben Hanson is going to turn back, free his condemned comrades and start where his brother left off. He has been radically changed and that change came from the God you refuse to believe in. You can see it written all over his face that he has been transformed. That is no act he's putting on."

"Well, maybe not…but if you're wrong in a month or so—we'll both pay dearly." Frank Arnon picked up his hat.

"And if I'm right?" Mr. Wellington pressed.

"I'll have to re-think what you've said. Goodbye, Michael, see you in a few months."

"Bye, Frank, and thanks a lot." The marshal shook the judge's hand and breathed a silent prayer for Frank as he left.

~~~

"What do you think, Will?" Mr. Wellington asked, stepping outside. He had arranged to meet the Bryant boys the next morning to see about the house.

"Well…I don't think that it'll be necessary to move everything out, just push it all to the far side of the house like the schoolroom, 'cause then it'll be out of the way and won't get damaged. It'll take a lot of clearing just to get where we can work things out for rebuilding. I think the earliest we'll be done is late spring."

"What do you think it'll cost?"

"Hard to tell yet. We'll do costs a step at a time."

"I wish I had time to do it myself—but the county's too big and I can't really hire another deputy. Let me know if there's anything you need." The marshal loosened his horse's tethers and headed out.

With tender and careful steps, Will and Stephen emptied Mr. and Mrs. Wellington's room of all its furnishings.

"This floor is really weak." Stephen's voice echoed in the empty room as they removed the last object. "The floor boards sag with every step, if you're not on the cross beams."

They left the other bedrooms upstairs the same, except for adding the extra furniture to a few of them. Downstairs, the sofa and easy chair were moved into the schoolroom, as well as the rocking chair and big braided rug. The piano had to be left alone, but the bench was moved. Tending to the kitchen took the rest of the day. William and Stephen got some crates and filled them with the surviving dishes and kitchen wares. The almost completely burned table and chairs splintered as they were dropped on the snowy ground, marking the spot for future debris.

"What do you think we should do with the stove?" Will asked. It was the last thing standing.

"Umm…well, it just needs a good clean up and it'll be as good as new. The pipe runs up and helps warm the bedroom…I think we should leave it until we knock out the wall, 'cause it probably won't fit through one of the doors, and the pipe will come down with the wall since they're secured together."

"Probably the best way. We can start tearing down tomorrow. I think we'll need Danny. But we should get home to do chores before supper." Will opened the front door, which was barely staying on its hinges. Stephen followed him out.

Lily—A Legacy of Hope 47

~~~

Life was different for the Wellington children. The house was a little crowded, but no one seemed to mind. School was done around the kitchen table. The girls loved helping prepare things for Alice's coming baby and the boys were always anxious to explore the new surroundings.

"Lily, would you take this crock of stew to the house for Danny?" asked Mrs. Wellington, on a freezing cold day.

"Sure, Mama."

"Thank you—he got so cold yesterday that he asked if we could bring him some warm lunch. So I just filled this crock with enough for all three of them. Here are some bowls and spoons, too. Oh, and take a jar of milk."

"Okay," Lily got her coat and boots.

The walk was so cold that it made Lily long for some of the hot stew that she carried. Danny, Stephen and Will were making a lot of progress in pulling down the charred timber.

"Oh, hi, Lil," Danny greeted, after they had brought a wall down with a tremendous crash.

"Hi! Here's the warm lunch you requested."

"What is it?" Danny relieved her of the heavy crock.

"Stew—Mama sent enough for Stephen and Will, too." She handed him the bowls and jar of milk.

"Oh, really? Where's theirs?" he teased.

"You're holding it. So how much is left to take down?"

"Well…just the stairs and the kitchen floor, then we'll pick it up and toss it in the pile over there. So tomorrow we can probably start getting ready to build."

"That's good. Well, you should eat before that stew gets cold. Oh, and Mama says to be sure and remember the dishes. They're Alice's you know."

"I will."

"See you at supper," Lily turned and started home.

"Bye, Lil." Danny brought the hot meal to his companions and they enjoyed it on the stone foundation.

~~~

Rebuilding went slowly, but steadily. The cold was a great hindrance. Danny was often working with Stephen and Will. A third pair of hands was constantly needed. On the days that it snowed too hard, Stephen and Will worked on the table, chairs and cabinetry. In April, as the weather warmed, progress increased.

Late in April, Mrs. Wellington took everybody over to the house to plant the garden.

"Why did Papa plow the garden bigger, Mama?" Jane queried.

"Because we're going to have to plant more to have a bigger supply this winter. It's not going to be an easy year after having to rebuild almost half of the house."

The garden was almost twice as big as its usual size. Everything was sown in double quantities.

"Well, if this doesn't get us through the year, I don't know what will," declared Olivia, covering her row of peas.

Planting took three days. Then they planted Alice's smaller garden, which was still considerably big. By the end of the week, the girls were tired of dirt and lugging buckets of water for the new seeds.

"It's done!" Mr. Wellington and Danny walked in the house one evening in early June.

"The house?" Jane was the first to meet them. The others were not far behind her at their father's voice.

"Yup," Danny affirmed.

The next day, the Wellington family moved back into their home. Luke and Alice gave a party to celebrate the day.

"It was so wonderful to have you stay with us," Alice told Mrs. Wellington before they left.

"It was wonderful to be here. Especially, for a few very important months." Mrs. Wellington embraced her before climbing into the wagon.

"Goodbye!" Luke and Alice waved as the family drove down the road.

"The house sure is going to feel empty," Luke commented.

"Not for long…" Alice gave him a bright smile, which he returned with a kiss.

~~~

"How much do I owe you for the labor?" Mr. Wellington walked along the main street of Oakville with Stephen and Will Bryant. In the passing months of building, they had given him the lumber bills out of honesty, hoping that he would overlook the cost of labor.

"Really, you don't owe us anything, Mr. Wellington," Stephen told him.

"I owe you a lot. Name your price."

Will and Stephen looked at each other.

"Okay, twenty-five," Will consented.

"Thirty-five." Mr. Wellington tried to persuade them to take more.

"No more than thirty."

"Thirty-five, I insist. Besides, the portion I received from Hanson's bounty money will cover it perfectly."

With funds being used up for the house, the month of June was tight for the Wellingtons. They tended the garden carefully, rebuilding the fence to hinder rabbits and other animals. In August, the girls went farther into the berry patches. It was not terribly hard to be frugal. Michael and Rachel Wellington had raised their children to be thrifty and they had never lived loosely, or been wealthy. There was no drastic change in life. They trusted in God and He proved faithful.

~~~

"Oh, Rachel, I'm so happy and so frightened at the same time." Ellen Barton sat at her kitchen table, visiting with Rachel Wellington over a cup of tea.

"What is it, Ellen?" Mrs. Wellington looked concernedly across the table at her friend.

"Well, I'm expecting."

"Oh, that's wonderful!"

"I know and I'm so excited. I'm just a little worried. It's been eight years since I've given birth. I'll be forty-two when he or she is born. I so want to bare Tom a child—and he wants one so bad. He's so excited. I'm just a little nervous."

"'Be anxious for nothing.' We will pray that everything goes well. I'm so happy for you, Ellen." Mrs. Wellington squeezed her friend's hand.

"Thank you." Mrs. Barton returned the gesture.

Chapter 4

On a hot July afternoon, Mrs. Wellington collapsed on the kitchen floor with a loud groan.

"Mama!" Lily heard her mother's cry of pain from the sitting room where she was working with Jane on their piano lesson. They rushed to where their mother lay prone on the floor.

"Mama, what happened?" Jane knelt by her mother, who was gasping for breath.

"I don't know—but—something seems terribly wrong…" She winced in pain. "Lily, I need you to hurry—get Papa and Dr. Barton."

Lily wasted no time in obeying. Saddling Amber seemed to take too long. So did the ride. Finally, she breathlessly burst through the door of the clinic.

"Dr. Barton!"

"I'm here." The doctor came out of back room with Danny.

"It's Mama. She just collapsed on the floor—and she's hurting," Lily choked back her tears.

"Get your father, Danny." Dr. Barton left with quick strides.

"Come on, Lil!" Danny led her outside, helped her back on Amber and then mounted Thunder.

Despite their efforts, Lily and Danny couldn't hide the fear in their faces from their father.

"I've got to go, Mark," the marshal barely said the words before he left with Danny and Lily in tow.

When they arrived back at the house, Mrs. Wellington was sitting on a kitchen chair.

"What's wrong?" Mr. Wellington hurried through the door and knelt beside his wife.

"I don't know." Dr. Barton paused and asked Lily to take her siblings outside. "But something's definitely not right," he finished, when they were gone.

"Do you have any idea what it might be, Tom?" Mr. Wellington asked.

"Not really. The baby's heart beat sounds a whole lot different from what it should be, though. It's irregular. I don't know what's happened, but from what I gather, you need to be on strict bedrest, Rachel. From there…I don't know."

Mrs. Wellington nodded. It wasn't going to be easy.

~~~

The next two weeks were difficult for everyone. Lily and Olivia took over all of the household duties. They had never realized how much work it was. On top of the work was school that they did in the parlor, where Mrs. Wellington rested during the day.

"Her condition is the same, but I still don't know what is wrong," Dr. Barton consulted Mr. Wellington alone one evening, after checking in on Rachel on his way home. "Since the baby's due soon, I think we should move Rachel to the Brockton Hospital."

"The hospital?" Mr. Wellington repeated in unbelief.

"There's something wrong and I don't know what it is. The Brockton Hospital is one of the very best in West Virginia. I think it's the best thing to do. If she or the baby has trouble, the best medical help possible will be right there."

"You're right…," the marshal nodded. His heart was heavy with troubles. How would they afford a hospital visit?

"We don't have to move her until Friday. She can see the week of school out, but we shouldn't wait too long."

"Thanks, Tom." Mr. Wellington shook the doctor's hand and said goodbye. Sadly, he turned and went back inside to tell his family.

"Everything will turn out fine," he tried to cheer their fallen and worried countenances.

Friday afternoon came, and with it many sad goodbyes. The Wellington children waved and watched as their parents drove down the road. The house felt hollow and empty when they returned inside. Everyone went about the rest of the day solemnly.

Luke and Alice stopped by on Saturday to help out and Mark, Pearl and Lucy visited on Sunday. It helped the children to have family around to help bear the burden.

On Monday morning, twin girls were born. But from the very start nothing went right. The labor had started late on Saturday night. It was unusually long and painful, but in addition to that, it was filled with grief. Faith was stillborn. Hope died soon after birth. None of the doctors understood why. In the short half hour of her life, Hope took only two breaths. Her parents watched in tormenting sorrow as she turned blue and left the arms of her earthly father to be caught up in the arms of her Heavenly Father.

With a very pale hand, Rachel Wellington tenderly touched the still faces of her little girls for the last time before they were taken from the room.

"Michael," she weakly whispered. "You need to go and tell the children. They need to know."

"Not until you can come with me." He held one of her hands.

"But that won't be for quite a while." She softly brushed his cheek with her free hand and squeezed the one he held.

Mr. Wellington gave in without any argument. He knew she was right. But he could hardly bring himself to leave her when her condition was so unstable. His aching heart could not bear the thought of losing his wife as well as two precious children.

~~~

"Papa's here!" Davy yelled from the window where he sat. Lily's head came up from the book she was trying to concentrate on reading to Peter.

Her toddler brother gasped audibly with excitement. "Mumma and Papa awr home frum da hostable?" In anticipation, they rushed to the door with the rest of their brothers and sisters. But their hopes were dashed when they saw that their father had come alone.

Mr. Wellington had just tethered his horse to the porch railing, when instantly all of them knew something was wrong by the look on his face. The marshal put his arms around Jane and Johnny, the closest to him, and led the way into the living room. Sitting down on the sofa, he tried to find the words.

"Your mother had twin girls," he finally forced it out. "Faith and Hope—Faith died before she was born—and Hope—Hope a little bit after."

It took a moment for the awful news to sink in. As it did, tears welled in his children's eyes and spilled down their cheeks. His own tears mingled with theirs.

"How is Mama?" Olivia finally asked through their crying.

"She's going to be in the hospital for a while yet. She's in a fragile condition. I'll ride back early tomorrow morning."

For a long while they cried, talked and prayed. At last, they all got up and went to do the evening chores. Sorrow filled the house through the rest of the night and the next morning when Mr. Wellington hugged his children goodbye and left once again.

Late in the week, Mr. Wellington returned with two little coffins and a small funeral was held. Their beloved mother's absence was obvious. Mrs. Wellington was still not strong enough to return.

Early the next week, word came from Mr. Wellington that Rachel had a low-grade fever. Friends often stopped by to help. Danny went back to work with Dr. Barton. He knew that some income had to be obtained to help pay the hospital bill. Stephen and Will Bryant were often around to help with the chores and the crop of hay that needed to be cut.

A second week passed and there was no change. Alice and Pearl often came by to help. It was obvious that Mrs. Wellington would be gone for an extended period of time.

"Hey, Livy!" Lily called one afternoon.

"Yeah?" Olivia came down the stairs.

"Do you mind if I run this basket to Grampa Charles, since Danny said that he hasn't been feeling well lately?"

"No, that's fine."

"I'll be back in time to do the wash and start supper."

"Okay, tell him hi from us," Olivia told her, as Lily went out the door.

The walk took some of the strain off of Lily's mind. It was hard to run a house even with the frequent help of Alice and her aunt.

With a swift step, Lily mounted the steps to the door of her grandpa's small house and gave a knock. She waited, but there was no answer. So she knocked again, calling for him.

"Grampa Charles, it's Lily."

No answer. Slowly, Lily turned the latch and the door opened.

"Grampa?" she peeked in the kitchen. No one. As she walked into the living room, the sight that met her eyes brought her to her knees. "Grampa Charles!"

Charles MacCrery's body sat glass-eyed and stiff in his rocking chair by the hearth.

~~~

"Danny?" Olivia walked into the barn.

"Over here, Livy." Danny came out from behind Amber.

"Could you do an errand for me?"

"What?"

"Lily forgot the get well pictures the little kids made for Grampa Charles. Could you run them over to him?"

"Sure," Danny saddled the horse he had just groomed.

Hearing a horse stop in front of the house, Lily looked out the window. Wiping her wet cheeks with the hem of her skirt, she sat hugging her knees at the feet of her deceased grandpa.

"Lil, Grampa…" Danny came through the unlatched door. "Oh, Lil…" he helped his sister to stand.

"He's gone, Danny!" Lily cried on his shoulder.

Danny tried to calm her down. Picking up her dropped basket, Lily allowed him to lead her out the door. He boosted her onto the horse and got on behind her.

"I knew it was coming, Lil," Danny confessed. "I just didn't think that it would be this soon. It was his heart—it was failing."

"I know, but why does it have to be all at once? First the twins, now Grampa, maybe Mama…"

"I don't know…but that's the way God wanted it. It's not a sad death, Lil, he was ready to go to see his Savior."

Lily could only nod because of the sob that was swelling in her throat.

"I know…this whole thing has been really hard." He tried his best to comfort her, although he felt as if he were speaking to himself more than to his sister. "God will see us through. He always has and always will."

By the time they reached home, the traces of Lily's tears had faded.

"I'm sorry, Liv." An apology was the first thing out of Lily's mouth when her younger sister came out the door.

"It's all right. Are you okay?" Olivia came down the porch steps.

Lily nodded, "Grampa's passed away."

"Oh, no!" Olivia's eyes moistened. She looked to Danny, who nodded.

"I'm going to run over to the Barton's and probably back to Grampa's—if you'll be okay. I should be back for supper." After the girls told him they'd be fine, Danny kneed Amber and rode away.

"Dead?" Stephen Bryant repeated.

"Yeah, last night I figure. His heart was failing. I was wondering if you guys might make his casket. I understand if you can't. I'm sure you're busy with other things…" Danny knew and understood that making coffins and digging graves brought back horrid memories for Stephen and Will. But they did it because they knew how much it meant for a departed loved one to have a final resting place known and marked.

"It'll be done tonight," Will told him.

"Thanks." Danny mounted and rode off.

"They sure are going through a lot of hard times." Stephen turned back to the barn.

"Yeah…"

"But their faith doesn't seem to be wavering and I don't think they've lost hope."

"I know, and if Mrs. Wellington has to stay in the hospital much longer, that may be all they have to hold on to," said Will.

For a while, they worked on in silence, each absorbed in their own thoughts.

"I've got an idea, Will…" Stephen leaned on his pitchfork.

~~~

The funeral for Charles MacCrery was a gray mid-September day. Mr. Wellington made it. When it was over, they visited the two small freshly filled graves that were just a few steps away.

"What's for supper, Lily?" Davy asked on the ride home.

"We'll see," she replied, quite unsure.

Lily looked despondently at the scant amount of food left in the pantry and cupboards. She wasn't sure how they'd afford to buy more. They'd have to really stretch the meals.

Lord, You've always proved faithful. Please provide for us and help us not to complain. Please heal Mama and bring her and Papa back soon.

Late that night, there was a loud knock on the door.

"Coming," Danny yawned as he went to answer it. He was baffled when he saw no one in the light of his lantern. "Hello?" he stepped forward. "Ow…" his foot bumped up against something rough and wooden. The small flame's glow fell on five crates of food goods sitting on the porch.

"Who's out there? Show yourself!" Danny shouted, confused.

Only the sound of crickets answered his call.

"Lily! Hey, Lily!" Danny shouted up the stairs.

"What?" Lily rushed out of her room and stood at the top of the stairs.

"Come and see!"

Lily flew down the stairs at his beckoning. "Oh, my goodness, where did all that come from?"

"Search me—get the others to help bring them in and put them away!" Danny picked up one crate and carried it to the kitchen, while Lily raced upstairs to rouse her siblings, who were just falling asleep.

"This feels like Christmas!" Jane cried, pulling out a small brown paper bag and opening it. Inside were licorice whips and jelly beans—enough for one each.

"This is probably enough for a month, if not more! Yum!" Olivia put the sugar and molasses in the pantry.

"I wish I knew who did it." Danny sat a sack of flour on the pantry floor. "They didn't even get just the basics; they bought sweets!"

"What an answer to prayer! We were really running out of things and I didn't know what we could do to re-stock." Lily stacked the empty crates by the door to be taken care of in the morning.

"I thought supper didn't taste as good as it usually does," Jimmy accused in a teasing way.

"You can still be grateful." Danny blew out the kitchen lamp and they all headed back to their beds.

~~~

"Lily! Olivia! Jane! Everybody!" Danny burst through the door, panting and yelling.

"What?" his siblings all filed out of the schoolroom.

"Papa sent a telegram! They're coming home tomorrow!"

The girls screamed with excitement and the boys jumped up and down.

"Did he say how she is?" Lily asked above the din.

"Weak, but she's okay and on the mend. The doctor said Mama could come home."

They spent the next morning in a whirlwind trying to clean up. In the afternoon, they had enough time to sit down and do their schoolwork.

"A wagon's coming!" Jimmy jumped from his seat. It had been a labor for all of them to concentrate on their studies. They stampeded for the door. Eleven eager voices spoke all at once as their parents stepped down from the wagon.

"Papa, you'll never guess what happened," said Jane, after they finished saying a long hello with lots of hugs and kisses.

"What?"

"God dropped food on our doorstep!" Sarah beat her sister to saying it.

"What?" Mrs. Wellington pulled off her bonnet as Mickey and Rachel led her into the parlor.

"Wait 'til I get back down!" Danny ran upstairs to put their parents' suitcase in their bedroom. When he returned, the story was told.

"Nobody knew how bad things were," Lily said, when it was done.

"What do you mean?" Mr. Wellington asked. Lily and Olivia had not told anyone how low their food supplies had gotten.

"Well…we were running out of food and were really making things stretch," Olivia answered. "'Cause what money Danny brought home went to the hospital bills—so we couldn't afford to go into town."

"Why didn't you tell me?"

"Because it was just another burden for you to carry—and there wasn't much that could be done." Lily looked at her hands.

A soft smile ironed out lines of care on Mrs. Wellington's face. "They know you too well, Michael."

"Yeah…" Mr. Wellington blinked tears from his eyes. "Let's pray…" Everyone bowed their heads as he began to give thanks to God for bringing them through the past painful weeks.

~~~

"Congratulations, Luke! You have a healthy boy." Dr. Barton walked out of the bedroom with a towel in his hands.

"Is Alice all right?"

"Well as can be. Go on in."

Melly Jane leaned out of her father's arms to get to her mother. Her small face was sober with worry. Alice's tired face glowed as she held out their newborn baby to Luke.

"What do you think we should name him?" Luke asked, as he gently adjusted the blankets to get a better look at his son.

"Andrew Michael," Alice promptly answered.

Luke looked up, the inward beauty of the woman he had married was again impressed on him. Andrew, in honor of his real father, and Michael for the man who had adopted him and loved him as his own.

"Andrew Michael..." Luke sat on the edge of the bed and kissed his wife.

~~~

Oh, Lord, help me to overcome my grief and give me joy for Alice's sake, Rachel Wellington prayed when she saw Luke's buggy pull up.

"Hello..." Alice hugged her mother-in-law when she came into the house. "I just wanted Drew to meet some of his family. You don't mind that I stopped by do you? I hoped it wouldn't be too hard..." Alice understood that it would be difficult for her to see Andrew so soon after the loss of Hope and Faith.

"I'll be all right. I can't hide from it. I'm so overjoyed for you and Luke. Are you doing okay?" Mrs. Wellington picked up Melly Jane.

"Oh, I'm fine. I'm a little tired yet, but I couldn't stay down." Alice followed Mrs. Wellington into the sitting room.

"And what do you think of your new baby brother? Do you like him?" Mrs. Wellington asked Melly Jane.

The three-year-old smiled and nodded in a toddler's jerky way, "I love baby brodder."

"She's been perfectly enamored with him. She barely held still when she got to hold him."

"I'll bet."

"Do you want to hold him?" Alice softly hesitated.

Mrs. Wellington nodded, readying herself for the pain. Andrew was gently passed from his mother to his grandmother.

"Hello, Little Man," she softly crooned to him, lovingly watching the big blue eyes and the little hands. An involuntary tear dropped to his soft blankets. "This is rare—I get a newborn who's wide awake. It was so sweet of you to name him after Luke's two fathers."

"Well, I liked the names and I knew it would mean a lot to Luke. I don't know how you did it. If Andrew died, I think I might curl up and die right along with him."

"If it ever does happen—which I pray it won't—God will give you the grace to go through it. If it weren't for Him and the rest of my family, I think I would have lost all will to live. It hurts—more than any other hurt I've felt—but I have peace knowing they are with God. I'll see them again. Besides, it's perfect for them to be with Him before us…our hope and faith lie in God—and He is what makes heaven—heaven."

Alice agreed with a loving smile.

"We're back and ready for history, Mama!" Jane and the others came in the back door a few minutes later.

"History is delayed, Love. We've got company," Mrs. Wellington smiled when she saw her children's astonished faces. None of them had heard the buggy arrive.

"Hello, Alice" and "Can I hold him?" circulated the room.

"You're so little," Lily cooed at her nephew when her turn came. It didn't last long, though, two other girls were excitedly, and somewhat impatiently, waiting for their turns.

~~~

"Susie, tell Mama that Will and I are going over to the Wellington's to meet Danny for hunting—we should be back for supper." Stephen cinched a leather sack closed.

"You're going over there again?"

"Just to pick up Danny, then we're hunting out in the fields west of there." Her brother brushed off her tone of annoyance.

"You've been over at the Wellington's so much in the past month and a half that I'm beginning to wonder if you even live here."

"Susie, you know as well as I do that they needed help running things over there. Danny had full days of work. Luke needed time with his family and Jimmy and Johnny couldn't do everything."

"Ready, Stephen?" Will came in the door.

"Yep," Stephen picked up his shotgun with the sack that held their lunch and left.

"Oh, my!" Mrs. Wellington admired, when she saw the bunch of birds Danny brought home that evening. Three pheasants, a goose and a grouse.

"We hit quite the patch of game," Danny put his shotgun in its place over the door. "Will and Stephen got three geese, two grouse and a couple pheasant. Well, I'll go string these guys up."

~~~

"Is's mo'ning. You weke?" Peter's charming voice broke through the sweet silence of Lily's sleep, as his little fingers touched her face and tried to pry open her eyelids. Resistant to the two-year-old's sweet annoyance, Lily turned her face away with a smile all the same. "Happy birthday, Lily! It's time to get up!" Danny jumped on the mattress with all fours. Peter was right alongside him.

"Oh, stop it! You're going to break the bed! Okay, boys, you've had your fun, now get off." Lily and Olivia pushed them. Caught off balance, Danny landed on the floor with a thud. Peter laughed, feeling triumphant that he'd managed to stay on the bed.

"Better calm down up there," Mr. Wellington's voice came through the wooden boards.

Lily blinked a tear out of her eye as she dressed. She suddenly didn't want to turn nineteen. She didn't want to grow up and get old. She wanted to be little again, like Peter. Life was so much easier when she was a little girl. *It's strange, when you're little you long to be big and grown up—when you become grown up you want to be little…never content…* the sudden thought disturbed her. *Lord, am I not content with my position and situation?* She didn't like the answer she found. She was content with her family, home and possessions, but in the past few months she had grown weary of all the burdens she had had to bear, and she'd begun to envy others for their seemingly easy and untroubled lives. The days had become monotonous and she had longed for something new and different to do. During the same old chores, she'd find herself daydreaming about greener grass on the other side of the fence.

Lily sat on the bed. *I'm sorry, Lord, I have been discontent and ungrateful. I've lost my focus on You. Please forgive me and help me to be content.* She felt the joy of God's presence fill her soul again.

Chapter 5

"Here, take this. You'll need it. I can buy another." Ben Hanson handed Jack Thomas the Bible that Marshal Wellington had given him half a year before.

"So long, Ben, I'll never forget what you've done," Jack shook his friend's hand.

"Good-bye, Jack, keep on preachin' the Word."

"You can count on it. I'll be seeing you when I get out." Jack Thomas shook his hand one last time and then watched as Ben Hanson disappeared out the heavy iron door that secured the outer courtyard of the West Virginia State Prison.

With a discouraged heart, Ben made his way through the winding corridor to the front of the prison. His heavy footsteps echoed on the stone walls. *I don't understand why, God, but I'm trusting You*, he thought, his mind wandering to the day before when he had been called to the warden's office.

"Can't keep you here anymore, Hanson," the warden had said.

"Why not? What have I done?"

"You cause too much commotion. I've had several complaints from the guards about your bold preaching. 'Sides, that Ray Trent is even more violent when you're around. Why they didn't hang him I'll never know…but you can't stay here any longer. You have to leave tomorrow and that's final."

"Are you opposed to me?" he had asked.

"Not in particular. Never thought religion hurt anybody, but it can get to be too much. So for your personal safety and for the sake of our sanity—I'm making you leave."

"This ain't just religion. This is bringing mankind back into a relationship with God—the way things were meant to be—by simple faith in Jesus Christ, the Son of God."

"I won't argue with you, Ben. I want to part on good terms. I'll see you at the gate tomorrow morning."

Ben sighed as that gate opened now and he walked out. It was thirteen long miles to the nearest town. Most of the terrain, in which the prison was deeply set, was the hill country of the Appalachians.

The sun had gone down when he reached the outskirts of the large town of Lyndale.

~~~

Brushing in mild frustration at loose strands of her bright red hair, Emily Burgess let out a weary sigh as she left the kitchen to answer the knock on her front door. For almost three years now, she had been running the boarding house she'd inherited from her parents, and was barely able to handle all the work it took to keep the place running.

Lord, I don't know how much longer I can take this! her mind cried, as her hand turned the door knob.

"Hello, may I help you?" her tired voice met Ben's ears.

"Ahh, ev'nin', Ma'am, I was wonderin' if you had room to board," he removed his hat.

Not another one! But then Emily saw his worn clothes and tired face and she couldn't say no. "I have an empty room. Please come in." She noticed that he carried no bag.

"I can't pay cash, so I was wonderin' if you had wood choppin' or other chores that I might do to earn my keep until I can find a job and pay you." Ben twisted the brim of his hat.

"That'd be fine. I'd really appreciate the help just as much as money right now. I'll take you to your room," she informed him, her deep green eyes smiling.

Ben went to bed with a satisfied stomach that night. He couldn't remember the last time he'd eaten so well. The soft bed felt strange after seven months on a hard prison cell cot.

In the morning, he went to the forge that was in the middle of town. It was the only trade he knew. A tall thickly-built man was bent over an anvil, swinging a ten-pound hammer.

"Howdy," Hadley Jones looked up. "What can I do for you?"

"I'm Ben Hanson, I was wondering if you might be lookin' to hire," Ben stepped closer.

"Might be. Had any experience?"

"Yep."

Peering through small green eyes, Jones took in the looks of his prospective employee. Not much could be said for Ben's appearance. His clothes were worn and his face was unshaven. But underneath the thin shirt was an obviously strong muscular upper body.

"Hmm…" Jones thought a moment. "Show me what you can do. Here's the sample." Jones set a metal strip on the work bench.

Ben looked at the flat strip of iron that had been twisted for a part in a gate he guessed. After eying it a minute, he turned to the rod that was about a half-inch in diameter and four feet long. The blacksmith had just started to flatten it to a quarter-inch thick.

"Would you mind pumpin' the bellows?" he asked, pulling on a leather glove then inserting the iron rod into the red embers.

"A good smithy oughta be able to man everything by himself."

Ben saw that Hadley Jones was a tough man who knew his business. *Well, Lord, I know my business, too, but I haven't handled a hammer in years. Help me use it like I never let it out of my hand.* With a nod, he began to pump the bellows himself. His timing was rusty. The rod was ready to be hammered the second time he pulled it out. Quickly, he laid it on the anvil and swung the hammer. A rhythmic clanging responded to each stroke. Beads of sweat formed on Ben's forehead more from nervousness than from the heat and strain. By the third time he had to reheat the iron, the old rhythmic skill was returning to his hands.

Flattening the rod took longer for Ben than it would have six years before. He thought for sure he'd lost the job just by how long it took him to get used to using the tools again. But Jones wanted him to continue. He saw skill that was only out of practice.

Ben poked half of the rod into the coals. Hadley started to protest but held his peace, deciding to see what different method Ben had. The iron was bright orange when Ben pulled it out, almost too hot for good molding. He took the tongs and pinched the glowing end. Holding it vertically with the hot end up, he began twisting both ends with even force. Jones watched in amazement as the flat metal twisted into a perfect helix. Ben glanced at the sample he had been given to confirm how tightly the helix was to be wound. The barrel of water used for cooling hissed loudly as the rod was immersed into it. Ben pulled it out and felt it. It was still hot, but touchable. With a satisfied look, he ran his finger along the twist. Then he slid his glove on and inserted the other end into the embers.

Not fifteen minutes later, Hadley had the finished product in his hands turning it over and inspecting it.

"Never saw it done like that, Hanson, but you got it perfect as can be, and in less time, too. Took you a little bit to get the hang of flattening it—but otherwise you've got the skill…how long has it been since you handled a hammer?"

"Oh—about six, maybe seven years, I reckon."

"Long time," Jones commented and laid the rod next to its twin on his work bench. "I can use a man like you. Seventy-five cents a day is the best I can do."

"Sounds fine. I'll take it. This is an answer to my prayers." Ben praised God as they shook hands.

A month later, he was walking back to the boarding house. He was just passing the schoolhouse when he saw three children running towards a woman who was just entering the schoolyard. For a moment, he paused on the side of the street opposite them and watched. A smile slowly formed on his face. The image didn't leave him as he continued on his way. It brought back sad, but fond memories and a strange feeling he didn't know how to deal with.

"What are you looking at?" Emily asked, when she found him looking at her. He was the last one up. All of her other boarders had retired to their rooms.

"Ohh, I'm sorry. Not quite sure. I…ahh…I was just lost in thought, I suppose," Ben shrugged. "Tired I guess. I'd better turn in, goodnight." He stood and left the warm sitting room.

Emily watched him go. She had noticed something in his gaze that made her face feel warm. Ever since he had come, her life had not just been easier, but strangely much more cheerful.

Oh, Lord, don't let me get my heart wound up in it. He's just a nice man who You've sent to help.

~~~

"It's snowing!" Jane rushed down the stairs. They hadn't seen the sun in almost a week, but no flakes had fallen from the sky.

"Oh, thank You, Lord!" Mrs. Wellington joined her children at the window. They had been praying so hard for snow. It was the nineteenth day in December and the ground was still brown.

"Okay, children, time to finish school," she told them, after enjoying the falling flakes for a few minutes. Slowly, they took their eyes away and followed her back to the schoolroom.

The snow fell for the rest of the day and all through the next. After three days, the skies cleared and two feet of sparkling white snow covered the ground.

"Yahoo!" the boys yelled. It was Friday and all schoolwork and house cleaning was done. Mrs. Wellington had given the children permission to go sledding. There was a flurry of hats, coats and mittens as they raced to get out. The boys won, of course.

They returned home completely worn out after two hours of constant activity.

"After much thought and decision, your mother and I have decided that we are going to forego Christmas presents this year," Mr. Wellington said, that night as they gathered for family Bible reading.

"Why?" Davy asked.

"Well, for a couple reasons. The first one is we really can't afford it, and your mother has pointed out that it is a bit of a stress and gives us more things than might be necessary. I have realized that it can be and sometimes is distracting from celebrating God coming to earth as a man to die for us. I think we can easily get too caught up in thinking about what we have to give and especially what we might get," their father explained. Though most agreed, he could tell it was going to take some getting used to.

It was more than a week before the Christmas Ball and the girls were excitedly discussing and deciding on their apparel for the occasion.

"I'm sorry, Livy, but we'll just have to make this dress do," Mrs. Wellington motioned helplessly with her hands. "There are plenty of tucks we can undo and the hem can be let down enough so it will look just fine."

"Oh, Mama!" Olivia pleaded.

"Livy, there is no possible way that we can afford a new dress. We can alter and adjust this one so it'll look like new."

"Don't worry, Liv. I have a few ideas that will make it look like a whole new dress," Lily tried to encourage her sister. Olivia only sighed.

The next morning while the others were doing schoolwork, Lily followed through with her promise. She laid the dress out on her bed and started letting down the hem. She was just finishing redoing it when Mrs. Wellington called for her to help with lunch.

"What are you doing with the measuring tape around your neck? Is it your new necklace?" Jane asked, when Lily came through the door.

"Oops!" Lily laughed, pulled the strip off her neck and ran it back upstairs to their room. "Is Livy done with school yet, Mama?" she asked on her return.

"Yes."

"Oh, good, I started on the dress. I let down the hem as far as it can go, so I have to see if it's enough."

Just the hem wasn't enough, so Lily had to take more length from the waist. While she was at it, she let it out as much as was needed. Nevertheless, a small amount of length still lacked.

"Hmm…what do you think about bordering the bottom with lace, Mama?" Lily questioned as she paced back and forth thinking, while she gazed at her modeling sister. By that time, Mrs. Wellington had also joined the project.

"That would make a nice touch—but all I have is remnants. None of them would be long enough to go around."

"Oh…" Lily's brows knit and Olivia's hopeful expression faded. "I think I have something." Lily darted out of her parents' room.

"Oh, no, Lil, not that!" Olivia looked horrified at what her sister returned with.

"Why not?" Lily insisted. "This petticoat was new last year and it's the perfect ivory to match the rose color. Not to mention that it shows no signs of wear. Nobody will ever know if this lace came from a petticoat—except us three. Besides, petticoats do not need lace. It's almost a waste."

"But that's the petticoat that I was going to wear under it."

"Well, who's going to care? What would you rather have? Lace on a petticoat that no one will see, or on the dress to make it perfect?"

"It's a pretty thrifty idea," Mrs. Wellington agreed.

Olivia shrugged her consent and Lily picked up the scissors and began to sever the lace from the petticoat. There was not time to sew the lace to the dress until the next day. When Olivia saw the result, she was glad Lily had insisted.

The other alterations to the bodice did not take long and Olivia's eyes glowed when she saw how transformed the dress had become. Half sleeves cinched at the elbow with a few lace scraps replaced the full sleeves, new tucks and darts flattered the whole style.

"Oh, thank you, Mama! Thank you, Lily!" she hugged each of her seamstresses in turn.

~~~

"All right!" Ben collapsed on the bed. He was weary of wrestling with God. For the past month, God had been prodding him to court Emily Burgess. Out of fear of his past, Ben had dug his heals in and refused to budge. The last week had shoved him over the edge.

I'll do it, Lord. I'm sorry for being so mule-headed...I still just don't understand. I won't lie to You, God, I like her—a lot, but even so, You're goin' to have to do a lot of work 'cause no woman would ever consider marrying me—not when the truth about my past comes out—which it will have to sometime...I won't lie to her about it.

The next evening, he discreetly waited for the other boarders to retire. But when they were alone, his tongue seemed to shrivel up. Emily sat softly humming in her rocking chair as she industriously knitted away.

"It sure was nice of the Johnson's to invite us to their Christmas party next week," she tried to make some small talk. Ben could barely grunt his agreement. She made several more attempts for conversation, but they all failed. Ben continually stared into the flames of the fire, still searching for the words to say.

"Ben?" Emily's needles paused mid-stitch. "Ben? Is everything all right?"

He looked at her then. With a deep breath he just started talking. "Emily, I've got to make a clean breast of this. I've just got to spit it out, 'cause I don't know how else to do it." He nervously moved his hands in a motion like he was slowly washing them. "I'm an outlaw," he expected her to gasp, scream, anything, but Emily sat looking at him, her green eyes calmly welcoming him to continue. "I'm George Hanson's younger brother. I'm the Ben of that gang. I was top dog with him for a while."

An almost inaudible gasp escaped her throat then. But she was still calmly waiting for him to continue.

Ben was stumped. She was doing everything exactly opposite of what he had expected her to do. "Y-you're not afraid of me? Why aren't you screaming for me to leave?" He was at a total loss for words.

One side of her mouth lifted forming a crooked smile. "Those are merely words, Ben, simply a—a past, I—there is no sense in my being afraid of you. We've talked openly of our faith—we walk to church together—you're my handyman—the answer to my prayer that God would send someone to help. The Ben Hanson I know is a man of faith—honest, openly kind and ready to extend his helping hand and friendship."

"My past doesn't affect you?"

"No! And I don't think it should affect you either. In fact, I might even venture to say that you are very blessed, in a way—because you truly know the debt of love we owe to Christ. You fully understand the depravity of man and what a huge love God has given us in forgiveness."

Ben was too awed to speak. He was completely stunned at her response and how God had moved. *I'm sorry, Lord, I should have trusted more fully that if this was Your will, it would take place and I had nothing to fear.* His gaze returned to the fire.

Emily silently continued her knitting, taking account of her words, hoping that they had not betrayed the feelings that she had sought to stifle for so long.

Ben broke the long silence that had ensued. "For a whole month, I've lived in disobedience to God—in fear of the pain I'd feel in damaging—our friendship."

Surprise registered in Emily's eyes as she looked up. But as suddenly as it had come, it disappeared.

"Emily, I would like to court you, if that's possible."

"You mean it?" her eyes were large and bright in the firelight. No man had ever called on her. It had deeply hurt her, but she'd learned to be content in being single.

Ben nodded. "I mean it with all my heart."

"I'd like that," a hesitant smile played about her lips. "I'd like that very much." She was not strikingly beautiful, but she had a pleasant face. Inward beauty radiated through it, making it very lovely.

"Well…I s'pose I should turn in. I'll see you in the morning," he rose from his chair and left the room. Emily's gaze followed him out of the sitting room and up the stairs. *Oh, Lord, You are so wonderful to me! Thank You!* Her heart sang.

~~~

Lily picked up her cloak, made a final glance in the mirror and hurried out of the bedroom. Danny helped her into the sleigh.

"I'm not the last one, for a change," she commented with relief, settling down beside Jane.

"Nope, it's Papa this time." As soon as Danny had said it, Mr. Wellington came out the door.

"I'm here."

The Evans' home was impressively decorated as always. Lily loved the warm glow that all the many candles produced.

"Hey, Beth…" she gave her friend a quick hug.

"Hi, Lily, isn't it just perfect?"

"It's always perfect."

"Why, thank you," Mrs. Evans came in on their conversation. "Lily, I was wondering if you would do me a favor."

"Sure, Mrs. Evans."

"Sally Tern usually plays the piano, but she's can't come, she's sick. So I was wondering if you might fill in for her."

"I'm not as good as Miss Sally…" Lily really wanted to but she didn't feel adequate.

"I doubt that. Would you please just try?"

"Yes, ma'am," Lily nodded.

"Oh, thank you. The sheet music is on the piano, so just feel free and do whatever. Maybe you want to run through it while hardly anybody's here…"

"Okay."

"Well, come on, Maestro. I think I'll help you with your repertoire," Beth joked good-naturedly after Mrs. Evans had moved on.

"Oh, that's funny—especially since you're not the one going to be tortured by your nerves," Lily grinned with good humor.

"Ed and Claire are engaged," said Beth, as they sat down together.

"Really?" Lily pulled out a piece and scanned it. Ed Nelson had been courting Claire Farns for a while. "I'm so glad. When did he ask her?"

"Just yesterday and the wedding's planned for Valentine's Day. Isn't that romantic?" Beth sighed.

"Mm-hm," Lily chuckled quietly as she started to play a song. Though she made mistakes, she was able to recover easily enough. Lily was relieved to find that the music wasn't as hard as it looked.

"Are you our replacement?" Sam Thompson, the town blacksmith, asked pulling out his fiddle.

"For tonight," Lily answered through her concentration on the music.

More people arrived and the ball started underway. *Lord, please help me. I don't want to make a mistake and mess up the dances*, Lily prayed as they prepared to play the very first dance. The first few pieces were a little harrowing for her. She was worried about messing up. But she forced herself to relax, remembering that she was to be anxious for nothing.

"When will you be free to dance?"

Lily took a fleeting glance away from the music to see who the speaker was. "I don't know," she answered Douglas Collins honestly.

"Could you keep a slot open on your card?"

Lily nodded, right now her card was completely empty.

"Thanks." Douglas walked off.

Lily couldn't help but notice a strange change in the way Douglas acted toward her. When she had been younger, his attention had been thoughtless and selfish, sometimes sarcastic teasing. She had avoided him at all costs. More and more she began to see that he was treating her more like a lady. *Maybe he's finally growing up*, she thought.

"Lily?" Olivia came up behind her sister towards the end of a song late in the evening. "Do you want me to play for a while?"

"Do you want to? Because I'm fine playing the night away. You don't have to reprieve me, if you don't want to."

"I want to."

"All right." Lily finished the song with an arpeggio, pulled out the next piece and then moved away for her sister.

"Come on, Mickey, you get my first dance." Lily relieved her mother of looking out for the curious five-year-old.

"Okay," Mickey willingly went to his sister and followed her to a corner where nobody was. He grinned widely and giggled happily as he stood on her toes as she moved him around to the music.

"May I cut in?"

Lily stopped and turned around to face Stephen.

"Um—well, it's my turn to watch Mickey and keep him out of mischief. It wouldn't be fair to give him back to Mama…"

"I understand…what if Marie or Emma watch him?"

"All right," Lily consented.

She's always doing things for others, Stephen smiled, as he went to find his little sister. Marie was more than happy to take Mickey. Lily hoped to return to him after their dance, but it didn't happen. Douglas quickly spotted that she wasn't playing the piano. He claimed his dance as soon as Stephen's ended.

A little while later, she was looking at the spaces on her card that had been taken. She sadly realized that the name of Charles MacCrery would never fill its usual place on the paper.

"Are you okay?" Mr. Wellington asked, seeing her mellowed face.

"Yeah…I was…just thinking about how Grampa Charles always filled at least one dance on my card."

"Well, come on. I'll gladly take the extra one."

"Oh, Papa!" Lily smiled and took his offered hand.

The night progressed rapidly. Families with young ones were soon saying goodnight. Seeing the late hour, several others followed suit. All that were remaining were the young adults who were waiting for the sleigh ride.

"Well, the sleigh's outside ready and waiting for the folks who want to brave the cold," Mr. Peterson announced, standing at the ballroom door in his heavy fur-lined coat and big mittens. "So everybody help make this place neat and then get your wraps and we'll leave our host and hostess in peace."

A while later, they were all wishing the Evans' a Merry Christmas and filing out the door to the massive sleigh Mr. Peterson had fashioned out of two smaller ones. A team of four horses was required to pull it.

"It's so cold out here!" Olivia shivered. "I don't remember it being this cold."

"Come on, the back is the most fun!" Anna, Beth and Marylou pulled Lily and Olivia to the very last seat. Lily sat on the opposite side since only four could fit on a seat.

"I think you're going to be cold, Lily. Everybody else is heading for the front," Anna observed. "Funny because the back is the best!" But she spoke too soon.

"Here, Susie," Will brought his sister to the back. Lily scooted over to make room.

"Did Danny sit up front?" she asked Susie, for she had thought that he would have followed them.

"Yeah."

"Everybody ready?" Mr. Peterson asked.

"Not yet!" Stephen rushed to the back of the sleigh. "Can I fit in?"

"Yup," Will moved closer to Susie, who had to shift towards Lily. "Now we're ready!" The sleigh started forward and the bells on the harnesses began their jingling. There was no moon, and all the stars stood out distinctly against the dark indigo sky.

"I think the wise men had a lot of faith and patience," Lily commented.

"Why do you say that?" Beth queried.

"Well, because they must have followed the star for months, maybe even a year or two. It says in Matthew that they saw the young child, and they were not in a stable by then, they were in a house—can you imagine a star so bright that it could be seen in the day?"

"You'd have to make sure you didn't confuse it with the sun. Although I s'pose that wouldn't be too hard, since the star always stayed in the east and the sun moves," said Anna.

Beth mused out loud, "I've always liked the part where God told the wise men not to go back to Herod, but just to go home. I wonder if they'll be in heaven."

Lily agreed, pulling her hood closer around her head. The cold air hitting her face was stinging her ears and cheeks from the speed of the sleigh.

Susie sat in silence, listening to the girls talk on. She was becoming weary of constantly fighting against the overwhelming evidence about who God really is. She saw it everywhere around her. But she refused to bend. Her proud heart wanted to stay angry and bitter towards the One she blamed for all the bad things that had happened in her life.

Someone's voice broke out in the song "I Wonder as I Wander" and the others followed. They sang for almost all of the remainder of the ride.

"This is unusual. We're almost never one of the first people to get dropped off," Lily observed, as the lantern left burning in their kitchen window came into sight. "I like being some of the last ones."

"Come on, social butterfly—somebody's gotta be first," Danny heard her last sentence.

"Goodnight! Merry Christmas!" The three siblings called, waving to their friends as they rode away.

~~~

"Come now, let us reason together...though your sins be as scarlet, they shall be white as snow...though they be red as crimson, they shall be as wool." Susie gave a sigh of exasperation as she settled under her covers. She couldn't get the words out of her head. They had been read by her father at the supper table. Ever since then, she had not been able to forget it. No matter how hard she tried, the verse would always return to her mind.

Disturbed, she told herself, *It's all a lie!* But the only peace she got was when sleep finally claimed her and even then it was a fitful rest.

"Are you comin', Sue?" Stephen's voice rang up the stairs. "Everybody's waiting. We're going to be late for the skating party if you don't hurry up!"

"I'm hurrying!" Susie came clattering down the stairs. "My hair wasn't co-operating."

In late January, there was usually a large skating party on Willow Pond where Whisper Creek emptied.

A few people were on the ice when the Bartons arrived. There were a couple fires built—one for enjoying and the other to heat a large cast iron pot full of cider.

"Please, Mama!" Rachel begged her mother. "I want to learn how to skate!"

"I'm sorry, Dear, but I have to take care of Peter for now. Why don't you go find Lily and ask her." Mrs. Wellington shifted Peter in her arms. The two-year-old was heavily bundled up against the cold and he was quietly whimpering about the small burn he had received from the pot he was told not to touch.

With a heave of her small shoulders, Rachel set off to find her oldest sister.

"Lily…" Rachel tugged on Lily's skirt.

Lily turned from saying hello to the Barton girls. "What, Rachel?"

"Can you teach me how to skate?"

"Now?"

"Yeah."

"All right, come on. I'll see you later," Lily waved as Rachel led her away. "Do we have skates small enough for you?"

"Mm-hm, Sarah's old ones."

They got their skates from the sleigh and sat down on the makeshift benches that consisted of log sections supporting planks of wood. Lily knelt in front of her five-year-old sister and laced up the skates Rachel had eagerly put on.

"Now hold on. Wait for me to get mine on." Patiently, Rachel swung her feet as she waited.

"Okay, here we go. Careful!" Lily caught her before she hit the ice. "You push off with the side of the blade like this," she demonstrated. "Now I'll hold onto you while we do it together." Lily put Rachel in front of her and said "right" and "left" each time she pushed off with that foot. At first, Rachel just stiffly watched as she began to move with Lily, but after a minute she attempted it, stumbling several times.

"Wanna try it on your own?" Lily asked, sensing after a while that Rachel was a little tired of constantly being held up. The little girl nodded. Rachel glided for about eight feet, but as she got ready to push off again, she lost her balance and tumbled to the frozen surface.

"That wasn't bad. You'll get better as you practice." Lily came to her rescue and helped her up. Lily marveled at Rachel's perseverance. She tried several more times before stopping to rest.

"You've gotten better with each try. You can't expect to be good right away," Lily said, noticing her little sister seemed crestfallen.

"Come on, Lily," Anna finished lacing her skates and wobbly stood up. "I'll race you to the other side."

"Okay, ready? Go!"

Anna won. Lily couldn't stop, so she crashed into the snow bank. Amidst struggling to get up, Lily heard a small ripple of laughter from others.

"Can you give me a hand, Anna?"

"Sure." Anna held out her hand and assisted Lily back to the ice.

"I never was a very good stopper," Lily said ruefully. "See, Rachel, I crashed and I've skated for years."

"You looked funny," Rachel giggled, her dimples showing.

"I'm sure I did," Lily laughed, too.

"Hurry up, Beth!" Anna was the first to see the Farns' arrive a few minutes later.

"I will!"

"Let's get Claire and the others, then we can do a pinwheel," Beth sat down on the bench and removed her boots. The pinwheel was one of the girls' favorite things to do on the ice.

There were four or five girls in the center holding hands and then others would link on to their other arms and they'd skate around like a revolving pinwheel. They would keep accelerating until the arms would break apart and the girls would fly off in different directions, like several 'crack the whips' at once.

"Everybody ready?" Claire asked, when the girls had formed the shape. She was in the middle with Anna, Susie and Marylou. "Go!"

Jane was the first to go. Her blade skipped on the ice and she wasn't able to recover. Emma did not last much longer. Lily managed to stay on for a while. But her legs became weak from constant strain to keep up with the fast pace the inner girls had chosen. She tried to hold on until there was a good place to let go. Her hand slipped out of Olivia's and she was sent reeling back to the snow bank where she had crashed before.

"I guess I'm just bound for that snow bank today," she told Jane, who came to her rescue. "Look out!" Lily grabbed Jane and rolled over, keeping both of them from being landed on by Beth.

"Sorry! I couldn't steer!" Beth got up and brushed the fluffy snow from her coat.

Two more times they did the pinwheel before everyone was too dizzy to try again.

"The girls said they can be done for a while so we can do some hockey, Danny," Stephen excitedly called. Danny smiled as he picked up his gloves and went to join the other guys.

The girls sat on the sidelines and cheered for the teams of their fathers and brothers. The first game was fathers against sons. With great effort, the fathers won. They had a re-match and the young men won.

"Your daughter's not cheering for you much, Nathan," Mr. Nelson teased Mr. Farns, as they lined up to play the tie-breaker.

"I know. Shows just how much she loves your son."

"Never doubted it for a moment, Nathan. They were made for each other." Ron Nelson gave his friend a slap on the back as both sides hunkered down, determined to win. The fathers' team claimed the overall victory.

When the darkness of night was too thick, families began grouping and heading home, tired and worn out from a day filled with fun and games.

Chapter 6

"Happy birthday, Emily." Ben reached in his pocket and pulled out a small box.

Emily looked up from the breakfast porridge she was cooking. Brushing her hands on her apron, she accepted the gift. Ben watched her expression with a mix of pleasure and hope.

Emily untied the twine bow on the little box, took off the lid and carefully removed the straw that hid the contents. On the bottom, lay a folded piece of paper. Her eyes widened as she unfolded it. It was an intricately woven silver ring. There was writing on the paper. Emily sucked in her breath as she read Ben's plain, bold script.

I love you, Emily. Will you marry me?

Impulsively, she crumpled the paper up with the ring still in it and brought it to her heart.

Ben's face fell. "Is something wrong?"

A smile lit up her whole face. "No, Ben. I would've married you yesterday and the day before…and I'll definitely marry you now! Will you put it on me?" she held out the wrinkled paper. Ben took it and unwrapped the ring from it.

"Do you like it?" he asked, as it slid perfectly onto Emily's left hand ring finger.

"It's beautiful. You made it at the smithy, didn't you?"

Ben nodded. "We had some scraps left over and Hadley said I could use them."

Emily's nose wrinkled. "Oh, no! The porridge!" She whirled around to the stove. The pot was starting to boil over. "Do you think Hadley would let you get the morning off?"

"If I had a good reason…"

"Well, I was thinking that after breakfast is all done, we could just go over to the church and have Pastor Dobkins do the ceremony right away. What do you think?" Emily turned around.

"I think we should do it!" He took both her hands in his. "I wish I had more to offer you, Emily…"

"God and you are all I need and want," Emily squeezed his hands to emphasize her words.

Ben turned to the cupboards, touched by her words. "I best set the table, our boarders will be coming down soon."

Emily's heart warmed with his change of words. Things would no longer be just hers and she rejoiced in that.

One of the boarders, Mrs. Hawkins noticed the glow on Emily's cheeks and the ring on her finger almost the moment she entered the dining room for breakfast with her husband.

"I'm so happy for you, Emily," she congratulated them.

Emily looked at the woman in surprise. "Thank you."

Mrs. Hawkins saw to it that the other boarders knew as well. She was a well-meaning woman and Emily enjoyed her friendship. When Ben came in from chopping wood and took his seat, Mr. Hawkins congratulated him. As he shook the man's hand and thanked him, Ben cast a quizzical look at Emily. She shrugged her shoulders slightly and looked at Mrs. Hawkins.

When the morning meal was over, Ben and Emily asked the Hawkins to be witnesses for their wedding and invited the other boarders, Mr. Simms, Miss Barkley, Mr. Tyler and Mr. Phillips to join them as well. All accepted.

Dressed in their Sunday clothes, the wedding party and their six guests set out to the church. Wearing church clothes was quite a sight for the middle of the week. The reason brought a large number to the church to join in the celebration.

"When I was little I never planned my wedding to be like this, but now I wouldn't have it any other way," Emily smiled as she saw the people gathering to follow them.

The ceremony was short, but it was beautiful and God-honoring. When they were pronounced Mr. and Mrs. Benjamin Hanson, the full congregation clapped as the couple kissed.

Hadley Jones brought round their cutter as the bride and groom walked down the church steps arm in arm.

"Newlyweds need to be by themselves for a while, take all the time you need," he shook Ben's hand.

"Thanks, Hadley."

"My pleasure."

Ben helped his wife up and then sat down beside her. Their friends waved as they drove out of the town for a sleigh ride all to themselves.

~~~

Olivia looked out the window and sighed. They were all bored. It was nearly a month after Ed and Claire's wedding. The fun of snow had worn off. It had come late and it was staying late. In mid-March, there was still a lot of snow on the ground and it had turned into dirty ice pellets instead of fluffy flakes. In areas where the sun shone on the ground, the ground was brown with dormant grass and mud.

"I'm ready for real spring," she sighed, turning back to her geometry assignment.

"I know," Mrs. Wellington sympathized, leaning over Jimmy to help him conjugate a verb.

Lily found herself fighting spring fever as well. Daily she would take care of Peter to free her mother for school, then she'd make lunch and often assist her siblings with piano practice, besides giving lessons. She battled having an idle mind and letting dreams consume her thoughts.

Oh, Lord, make me find You to be all my sufficiency, she prayed each morning.

Towards the end of March, the weather began to warm slightly, bringing rain to aid in melting the remaining snow. The ground was still muddy and the grass was just barely showing small signs of green when April arrived.

"Mama?" Lily peeked into the schoolroom after finishing the lunch dishes.

"Yes, Dear?"

"Since Peter's down for his nap and you don't need me to help with history and geography, could I go for a walk? I'd like to get out and see if the snow-drops and crocuses are blooming around Whisper Creek."

"You may go. That's fine." Mrs. Wellington nodded.

Happily, Lily put on her sturdy walking shoes and wrapped a light gray shawl around her shoulders. Getting outside into creation alone and letting her thoughts flow in prayer always refreshed her. A brisk east wind bit her cheeks as she stepped off the porch. *A storm's coming*, she thought half consciously. Her eyes lifted to the sky. There were a few small clouds, but the sun was out and she was barely able to detect a gray hazy line on the western horizon.

The ground was still soft. There had been plenty of rain early in the month. Lily made swift progress from the house to the rising hills in the southeast. The old and almost completely decayed leaves on the narrow trail aided her in avoiding the mud. The slope gradually steepened and her pace slowed along the winding path. Lily followed the small ridge for a while until it came to where the ground leveled off and dipped a little to form a cove.

As she had hoped, there were snowdrops and crocuses in rock crevices and sunny spots around the spring-fed pool where Whisper Creek began. This was one of her favorite places to be.

Lily sat down on a short flat topped rock and watched the spring incessantly gurgle with fresh water. After a moment, she bent over the surface and dipped her hands in it. The frigid water was crystal clear and the rocky bottom could be seen two and a half feet below the surface. For a long time she sat and took in the beauty of the pool and its out-flowing stream, peacefully babbling along.

Finally, she stirred and started to walk along the creek bank. The stream tripped and tumbled over smooth round stones and rough ones that it was still polishing. There was a rock in the middle of the creek where it widened and fell down in a miniature waterfall. Lily stepped on it, watching the water swirl and eddy below her feet. The loud rushing sound of a strong and gusty wind blowing through newly budding branches caused her to lift her head. In the shade of the woods, she had not noticed that the sky had become heavily overcast with ominously dark clouds. *Uh-*

oh! she thought, jumping to the other side of the creek and hurrying up-stream, the way she'd come.

Just as she came upon the pool, the skies opened and rain came pouring down. Lily broke into a run, wondering how the storm had come so fast. Rain came in torrents. Thunder rumbled in angry response to the lightning's eerie flashes. The already wet ground quickly turned into slippery, sloopy mud.

Lily was drenched when she reached the ridge. As she ran along the side of the rock ledge to start her descent, Lily's foot slipped on a wet tree root. She had no chance to regain her footing. Screaming, she fell down the steep slope, unable to grab something to stop her. The heavy rain seemed to lubricate the ground and everything within her grasp. Her fall came to a sudden stop as she dropped over the edge of a gully that the rains had made at the bottom. A cry of pain escaped her lips as her left leg was caught between a large stone and the side of the gully. It was painfully wrenched as she rolled over from the force of the fall.

Slowly, Lily recovered from the shock. Her teeth began to chatter from the cold rain that had soaked her through and through. With effort she sat up and removed her leg from the crevice it was stuck in. Using her right foot, she stood and took a step forward. The pain it caused her was excruciating and she collapsed.

"Oh, Lord, help me!" she cried out in the watery gully. Home was still more than half a mile away.

~~~

Mrs. Wellington looked with concern out the sitting room window. The rain was pouring down in thick sheets and lightning zapped across the sky leaving a constant wake of thunder. *Lily, where are you? Lord, please protect her...* She prayed just as she saw Danny rapidly come home and bring Thunder into the barn.

"Good gravy, did this storm rush in!" he said, when he came in the door.

"Danny, will you go back out and find Lily?" Mrs. Wellington came to the door.

"Lily's out in this?"

"She went out walking by Whisper Creek before the storm came. It started half an hour ago and we haven't seen her. I'm afraid that something's happened."

"I'll find her. She was going up to the spring?"

Mrs. Wellington nodded and stopped him from putting on his wet coat. "Let me get you a heavy sweater and a rain slicker instead of this sopping thing. You'll catch your death otherwise."

Danny waited with a smile at how she always took care of her eleven children, seeing to each one's needs individually.

"Thanks, Mama. Don't worry, I'll find her. I know those woods like the back of my hand. It won't take long." He pulled the sweater over his head and followed it with the slicker she brought him.

~~~

With tremendous effort and pain, Lily crawled up the hill and slid down through the woods into the meadow that was south of the house. Completely exhausted, she kept forcing her stiff joints to move. Almost her entire body was numb with cold. At least it helped reduce a little bit of the pain she felt.

"Lily!" in the pause between grumbling thunder, Lily heard a faint voice.

"Here!" was the only word she could utter through lips she couldn't feel. "Here!" she tried to raise her voice above the low rumbles of the sky.

"I'm coming!" Danny heard and saw her. "I'm here. What happened? Are you all right?" he knelt down and picked her up.

"F-fell in a g-gully. B-broke m-my l-leg," Lily couldn't stop her teeth from chattering.

Mr. Wellington was standing, waiting on the porch when he saw Danny coming through the rain with Lily in his arms.

"What happened?"

"Her leg's broken." Danny walked up the steps and through the door his father had opened. Lily was passed from Danny to Mr. Wellington, who carried her to the sitting room couch.

"I'm going to the office, Mama," Danny told Mrs. Wellington as he headed out again. "I'll need some things there that I don't have in my saddlebags. Get her warm and dry as fast as you can. I'll hurry back."

"All right. Be careful."

With Olivia and Jane's help, Mrs. Wellington removed Lily's dripping clothes and dressed her in a flannel nightgown. She was shivering violently by the time they were done.

"Jane, would you go heat some water for tea? We need to get something warm into her," Mrs. Wellington said, pulling the blankets over her daughter.

Jane quickly complied. Lily was just finishing her hot tea when Danny returned.

"It's your left one?" he asked, carefully lifting the blankets off of her feet.

Lily nodded. Her left leg was noticeably more pale and swollen than her right and the flesh felt cold to Danny's touch as he felt the fracture.

"How is she?" Mr. Wellington came into the room as his wife quietly ushered everybody else out.

"She's got quite the break. I think struggling to get back home made it worse," Danny pulled out a glass bottle containing a brownish liquid. He picked up Lily's empty cup of tea, filled it almost to the brim and gave it to her. Lily choked on the first swallow.

"Oh, do I have to drink it? Ugh…it tastes horrible and burns my throat."

"I know, but it'll help you feel warmer and ease the pain. Drink it fast, then you can wash it down with water."

Gulping the amber liquid down, Lily obeyed, although every part of her wanted to reject the vile drink. The water helped erase some of the burn, but the aftertaste was the worst Lily had ever known.

"Okay, you ready, Lil?"

Pressing her lips together, she nodded. The tug Danny gave her leg was firm and sudden. Even with the sufficient dose of whiskey, the pain it caused Lily was worse than when she had first broken it, and the lips she had so firmly sealed against a scream involuntarily broke apart to voice just how much it hurt.

Her cry was well heard in the schoolroom where all the children were. With a terrified look on her face and tears in her eyes, Rachel ran to her mother. Mrs. Wellington jumped at her daughter's cry and looked down as her legs were tightly embraced by little arms. Gently, she disengaged them and picked Rachel up.

"I don't want Lily to die, Mama," Rachel's voice trembled as she held onto her mother's neck.

"Oh, Love, she's not going to die. Fixing a broken leg just hurts a lot." Mrs. Wellington looked at her other children, who had looked up with concerned and frightened faces when Lily screamed. "Let's pray children. That's the best thing we can do."

The intense pain continued after the leg was set and Danny began binding it up with a splint.

"It hurts so bad, Danny!"

"If it's too painful, I could give you some more—" Danny started to reach for his bag.

"No! Don't! Please don't!" Lily pleaded, willing to suffer pain more than the torture of that awful tasting stuff.

"Are you sure you'll be okay without it?"

"Mm-hm," Lily tried to relax, determined to endure the pain. All of her siblings coming in to see her and ask how she was, helped distract her a bit from the hurt.

After supper was finished, they played games in the sitting room, but Lily found herself rapidly getting tired. After a few games of checkers, she could hardly keep her eyes open. She fell asleep amidst cries of victory and despair as Danny had just won a game of chess against Johnny.

"Mama, Papa?" Olivia padded into her parents' bedroom in the middle of the night.

A light sleeper, Mr. Wellington rolled over first with a slight grunt. "What's the matter, Livy?"

"Lily's tossing and turning. I think she has a fever."

"Oh, no…" Mrs. Wellington slid out of bed and lit a lamp.

Lily's temperature was high and she fitfully stirred in a "fever dream." When gentle shakes and words didn't wake her, Mrs. Wellington left to get a basin of water.

"I'll bring her into Pearl's old room," Mr. Wellington told her as she left.

Lily woke with a start to the cold rag that her mother gently placed on her forehead. She sat up gasping and looking wide-eyed.

"Shhh…you're all right, Lil," Mrs. Wellington crooned softly, making her lay back down.

"Water—can I—have some—water?" Lily's face contorted as if she were in pain.

"Is your leg hurting?"

She shook her head restlessly as she tried to push down the blankets. Mrs. Wellington held her head up so she could sip the water. As her mother bathed Lily's face with water, her father knelt by the other side of the bed holding his daughter's hand and praying out loud.

"Father, my little girl is hurting, and there isn't much I can do to ease the pain. It hurts me to see her suffer so, and You know and understand the hurt a father feels for his suffering child. Will You please heal her? Ease the pain and help her to sleep deeply and peacefully the rest of the night. Give her comfort and true rest. Thank You for the precious daughter she is. In the name of Your Son, amen."

Eventually, Lily did fall asleep. But for her it felt more like falling into an achy subconsciousness.

~~~

"Pneumonia?" Ellen Barton looked at her husband with worry two days after the accident.

"Yeah," Dr. Barton sighed, as he set down his hat. He had just returned from the Wellington's, confirming Danny's dreaded diagnosis of pneumonia.

"Is she really bad?" Stephen asked.

"It's looking that way—things were finally calmed down and now this happens. Praise the Lord, though, their faith has not wavered one bit and if anything it's gotten stronger. But who can know what'll happen now…"

Susie sat in silence listening to her family as they continued talking. Another blow was given to her arrogant unbelief in God. In the past year so much had happened to the Wellington family that she couldn't imagine why they never wavered in their faith. She went to bed that night evaluating what her own family had lost a few years before. She didn't want to admit to herself that the Wellingtons had suffered just as much. While she had lost her little brother, father and had moved to a strange place, the Wellingtons had suffered the threats of an outlaw gang, a house fire, losing twins, their grandpa and almost Mrs. Wellington. She refused to think about what her heart was trying to say. *It's impossible! It's not because of God's love that they're staying strong. They're just so far into religion that they believe those lies about God! It's all in their imagination.*

~~~

Lily's chest heaved. She was exhausted from coughing and uncomfortable with the fever. She wanted to lie down, but it made breathing even harder and the coughing worse. The night had been miserably passed. She had no idea when or even if she had slept.

"How're you doing, Lil?" Danny came through the door.

"The same," Lily rolled her head to the side. "How much longer do I have to have this poultice on for? It stinks."

Amidst the serious situation, a smile played on Danny's lips. "For a while yet. I want to let it do as much as it can. Do you want some of Mama's perfume to lessen the smell?"

"No, that would make it worse. Having sweet smelling perfume with onions and mustard? Yuck—is Mama doing school with the others?"

"Yup," Danny sat in the chair by her bed. "So I'm your in-room nurse and doctor."

"Well, Nurse, would you please read to me?" Lily labored for another breath.

"What shall I read?"

"Isaiah."

"Isaiah what?" Danny picked up her Bible on the small table by the bed.

"43."

"The whole chapter?"

"Not if you don't want to, but don't stop before verse 21." Lily settled back, hoping she would be able to fall asleep to her brother's deep voice reading the Scripture.

"But now thus saith the Lord that created thee, O Jacob, and He that formed thee, O Israel, Fear not: for I have redeemed thee, I have called thee by thy name; thou art Mine. When thou passest through the waters, I will be with thee; and through the rivers they shall not overflow thee: when thou walkest through the fire, thou shalt not be burned; neither shall the flame kindle upon thee. For I am the Lord thy God, the Holy One of Israel, thy Savior: I gave Egypt for thy ransom, Ethiopia and Seba for thee. Since thou wast precious in My sight, thou hast been honorable, and I have loved thee: therefore will I give men for thee, and people for thy life. Fear not for I am with thee…"

The peaceful and poetic flow of God's Word, read with feeling by Danny, sent Lily to a peaceful sleep until the middle of the afternoon.

Lily's fever spiked and she was beginning to slip deeper into delirium. Phantom-like images appeared out of nowhere and danced across her vision. Some began chasing her in a menacing way. When Lily bolted up in bed shrieking for someone to save her, gentle hands would make her lay down again with a blur of a soft voice.

In a cold sweat, Danny watched his sister. He had never seen such a violent delirium. Lily's frantic mumbling was almost constant and she was mildly tossing under the blankets.

"I can't let her fever go any higher, or we might lose her completely. I need the ice *now*. Is Papa back yet?" Danny asked his mother, looking at his younger sister's flushed face. An opening and shutting of the front door gave them the answer. In a moment, Mr. Wellington and Dr. Barton were bringing the ice upstairs into the room and spreading it over a tarp covering Lily.

"What are we going to do for her breathing? She's barely getting enough air."

"Keep giving her water—it should be as cold as possible 'cause that will help take down the swelling from asthma—as well as thinning the mucous," Dr. Barton instructed.

"Call me if things get worse," Danny said, leaving the room. He felt like the whole day he had been taking every breath with his sister. Patiently, he had borne listening to her labored breathing for most of the day. He had been able to feel her strain for each inhale. Now with Dr. Barton available, there wasn't much to do, so Danny eagerly left the room. The fresh April air helped revive his senses as he sat on the front porch step. Putting his elbows on his knees and his chin in his hands, he stared at the woods a hundred yards away.

"We need a miracle, God. Spare her, Lord. Please don't take my little sister. I need her. We all need her…" Danny paused. It took a long while, but eventually he was able to say: "Nevertheless, Your will be done. It's too hard to let her go, but Your will must be done and may You be glorified in whatever You do." Understanding how great God is, he felt and knew he was completely helpless to do anything but submit to God's will. But he was determined to do so willingly, with no reserves. "Thy will be done."

Chapter 7

"Will, it's your turn," Susie impatiently drummed her fingers on the table, waiting for her brother to take his turn.

"Oh," Will absently leaned forward and randomly moved a piece on the checkerboard. Susie responded with a triple jump that ended the game.

"What's the matter?" Susie sighed with exasperation. "You hardly played the game. I've never beat you."

"Sorry, Sue, my mind is in another world. I should probably just go to bed." He picked up the checker pieces and put the game away.

Will went to his room, but he couldn't sleep. So after a long, futile attempt, he joined Stephen in waiting up for Dr. Barton. It was after midnight when their father returned. Wearily, the doctor quietly entered the house. Stephen and William both expectantly looked at him.

"It'll be a miracle if she lives to see the morning," Dr. Barton answered their questioning eyes. Discouraged, he slumped into a chair opposite his sons. "If she dies, it will be the third child

Michael and Rachel have lost in seven months. They're already crushed at the thought of it. I don't know what they'll do."

"There's no hope?" Stephen asked.

"With a physical doctor's ability, no." He halted. "But there is always hope with God," he added with a ragged voice.

"We'll just have to keep praying." Will laid a reassuring hand on his father's shoulder.

~~~

Susie came into her brothers' workshop the next day. "Lunch is ready, Stephen."

Her brother made no response from the chair back he was engraving. "Stephen?" she repeated his name.

"What?" Stephen finally looked up.

"Lunch is ready. Didn't you hear me?"

"Yeah, I was just thinking and praying—sorry."

"You and Will lately…what's with you? You're completely oblivious to almost everything."

"You understand why, Susie." Stephen took his leather apron off.

"Because Lily broke her leg and is dying of pneumonia," Susie's frustration came out in a sassy tone. "You'd think you were in love with her or something."

"You just can't see it, can you?" Stephen brushed off the taunt. "You're completely blind to what the Wellingtons are to us. They have been the best friends we could ask for. They're the ones who reached out to Mama and you while Will and I were in Virginia. And Lily's the one who helped save Will when he got shot in Richmond. Can't you see that the reason the Wellingtons are what they are is because of their belief in God? Why don't you just give in? Stop being so proud and stubborn. You can't possibly say that God doesn't love us. The Wellingtons are one proof of it. And you have rejected them and Him in a horrible way." Stephen walked out of the workshop, leaving her in angry frustration.

Susie was quiet all through the noon meal. Mrs. Barton tried not to notice.

"Mama, would you be able to come out to the shop and look at this chair back I'm working on? I'm wondering what a feminine eye will think of the design," Stephen asked his mother as the dishes were cleared.

"I'd love to. Leave the dishes for me, Susie. I'll take care of them when I come back in," Mrs. Barton told her daughter, going out the door.

"I'm wondering if the design is too masculine. I thought it was fine when I sketched it on paper, but it's turned out differently on the wood," Stephen held up his piece of work.

"Oh, no, it's beautiful. Sandy Ballister will like it," Mrs. Barton ran her finger along the smoothly engraved lines. "What do you have left to do?"

"Some sanding and refining of the lines, boring the holes and screwing the rungs, legs and seat together, then staining it. Mrs. Ballister wanted it stained dark, not lightly varnished."

"I hate to say this, but I think you and your brother have far outdone your pa."

"Well, he was a good teacher—what I'd give to talk with him one more time. I should never have taken his life for granted; should have told him I loved him more often." Stephen gritted his teeth against the rising feelings and memories that flooded his mind.

"He was good to us. I wish we could see him again, too. It's hard to let it all go. I'm thankful we can rest in God's promises and your new pa's love. It hurts me so much, though, to see your sister rejecting His comforting love."

"I know," Stephen swallowed hard, thinking of the lecture he had given Susie.

"Well, I best go do those dishes before Susie does them for me," Mrs. Barton put a smile on her face.

A little later, Stephen came into the house calling for his mother.

"Shhh," Susie hushed him from the kitchen. "She's just laying down for a nap."

"Can you help me then? Will's not back from Charlettedale yet."

Susie nodded and followed him.

"Hold this leg here while I screw it in." Stephen placed one of the four wooden legs in its place. Susie followed his instructions.

"You can talk to me, you know," he said after a while. "It's not fun working in silence."

"I don't want to interrupt your thoughts," Susie told him.

"You're not interrupting anything. I like talking with my family more than thinking silently to myself."

"All right. Why are you so worried about Lily?"

Stephen looked up from the screw he was twisting into place. "I thought you didn't like this subject. I'm trying not to worry about her—God tells us not to worry about anything—careful, don't press too hard. It's sliding a little and I don't want the screw to strip—I'm leaving Lily in God's will—whatever it may be. It's Lily's family I'm more concerned about. They've had a lot to go through. But I shouldn't worry. God always keeps His word and He says He won't try us more than we can bear. His grace is sufficient."

"There you go again! It's all about God."

Stephen made no comment, but finished securing the leg and moved on to the next one.

"Was Pa going to stop by the Wellington's on his way home tonight?"

"As always," she sighed complainingly. "I don't think it's good for him. Lily's been sick for more than a week. He's been taking it on as his own burden and he's often been staying late there. We need him here. He's home little enough as it is. They have Danny for a doctor if they need one. I don't think it's right for them to be taking him away from us so often."

"They're not taking Pa away from us, Susie. He goes there of his own will. He's a huge support for them. We should be there for them. That's what good friends do. They shouldn't have to go through trials alone. God wants us to help bear one another's burdens."

"When will you stop this religious talk?" Susie's voice rose slightly in frustration.

"When I'm dead and in the grave." Stephen handed her the next leg. His calm and decided answer irritated Susie even more. With all her might, she hit the side of his arm with the chair leg he had given her.

"Ouch! Susie!" Stephen looked up in surprise to glimpse hot angry tears falling down her face as she spun around and ran outside. He rubbed his stinging arm and went to meet Will, whom he heard returning.

"Well, I'm back. The order's underway, should be done in a day or two. What's wrong with Susie?" Will slid down from the saddle.

"She's mad at me," Stephen recounted what had happened, as they returned to the shop.

Forgetting that her mother was sleeping, Susie ran into the house, slammed the door and stormed to her room. With hot tears of anger, she sat on her bed and sobbed into her pillow.

Will walked up the stairs a while later and knocked on the door before he opened it. "It's me, Sue," he went in and sat on the bed when she made no reply. "Stephen told me what happened. I think—"

"I don't want to know what you think!" Susie screamed, using the pillow to hit him with all her might. "I'm sick of hearing what everybody thinks! I'm sick of hearing you and Stephen talk about God! And I'm sick of hearing you talk about the Wellingtons! Now just leave me be!"

Shocked and hurt, Will left her. Susie slammed the door behind him.

"What's happened?" Mrs. Barton demanded, seeing him come out.

"I think God's pressing hard on her, Mama." Will put his arm around his mother's shoulders and explained what had happened.

~~~

Lily's head slowly rolled over. She was shivering like a leaf in the wind. Every breath was shallow and raspy. Through the night, the blanket of ice that covered her had slowly lowered her fever.

Danny's quick eye noticed her movement. "Lil, Lil, can you hear me?" He knelt by the bed.

In a feeble attempt, Lily opened her mouth, but no sound came from her throat. Her jaw closed and she rolled her head to the opposite side in a despairing way.

"I'm here for you, Lil. Mama and Papa are trying to sleep, but I'm here. Do you think you could manage some water?" Danny barely caught the tiny nod of her head. It took a little while, but he managed to spoon feed his sister a little more than a cupful of water.

"I ache all over…can hardly breathe." Lily's voice was a whisper after her throat had been revived.

"I know," Danny's heart wrenched at the thought of helplessly watching her slowly suffocate. "Do you want me to read to you?"

Lily nodded. Talking took too much of her precious air.

"Isaiah 43?"

Lily nodded again. "After Psalm 69."

"Save me, O God, for the waters are come in unto my soul. I sink in deep mire, where there is no standing: I am come into deep waters where the floods overflow me. I am weary of my crying," Danny hesitated, the words echoed the agony of their hearts. "Mine eyes fail while I wait for my God…"

Like balm on burning skin, God's Word soothed Lily's mind away from her cold and aching body.

The morning dawned, and hard though it was, Lily was still breathing. Danny and Mr. Wellington removed the ice even though her fever remained. For the rest of her family, it was like standing on pins and needles, waiting for the end to come. Lily herself expected and longed for death, she was in such pain. She made sure that each and every one of her family knew that she loved them. Though she knew that they already knew it, she couldn't bear the thought of dying without telling them one last time. Through the whole morning not a single face was able to smile.

"Come on, children. Let's try to get some schoolwork done." Bracing herself, Mrs. Wellington led nine of her moping children into the schoolroom. They had spent the whole morning with Lily and there was nothing to do but watch and wait, so Mrs. Wellington wisely thought that they'd make use of the waiting time. The afternoon dragged on, but the children made a lot of progress in their lessons. They didn't feel like doing anything else.

~~~

"Oh, God, how could You love me?" Susie sobbed, after she heard her brother and mother walk downstairs and outside. "How could You love me after I've treated my brothers the way I did? I'm horrible! Just wretched! How could You love me?" Groping for some kind of answer, she reached out and picked up Emma's Bible. Desperately, she flipped through the thin pages. "Just show me the truth, God. I don't care what it is anymore! I just gotta know."

Her whole frame was racked with weeping by the time she stopped reading.

"Oh, Lord, forgive me! I'm horrible and full of pride. Please save me, I believe in You and Your love. I believe You died to save me, and—and I thank You for it. Thank You!" Susie felt the millstone of sin she'd been trying for so long to free herself from, loosen and leave her heart. God's perfect peace filled her soul.

After washing and drying her face, Susie went in search of her brothers.

"I'm sorry, for everything. I've…I've been so horrible! Will you forgive me? I know now and I believe. God's saved me."

Susie's meek words brought great joy to her brothers' hearts.

"Oh, Sue…it's all forgiven and forgotten." Will hugged her.

"Same here, Sis."

Susie smiled then.

Tears of joy overwhelmed Mrs. Barton when she was told.

"Thank You, Lord!" was all she could say as she embraced her daughter.

~~~

Late in the day, Lily's fever began to rise again. Danny decided against getting more ice, he wanted to let the fever do what it could.

"How is she?" Thomas Barton asked, when Danny opened the door for him that night.

"Alive, but her fever's rising again."

Surprise registered on Dr. Barton's face that Lily still hung on. If he hadn't known, he might've taken her for dead when he went into the room.

Lily exhaled a small and ragged breath. Danny, his parents and Dr. Barton watched in anticipation of the next. It was several moments before her chest rose. They were just relaxing, when the raspy inhale was suddenly stopped short by a strange percolating sound. Lily's lungs tried to inhale more, but she only managed a couple short gasps. Immediately, she was leaned forward by Dr. Barton. When he didn't hear the blockage clear up, he gave her a solid pound on the back, cupping his hand for it to be more effective. In response, the last bit of air her lungs had left was shoved out, clearing the airway. Breathing again, Lily began to cough. It was a croupy and convulsive cough that she couldn't stop. Quickly, it began to be productive.

"Take that basin and put it in front of her, Danny," Dr. Barton directed. For almost half an hour, Mr. and Mrs. Wellington watched with tears silently gliding down their cheeks and breaking hearts, as their daughter fought for every breath and the bottom of the basin was covered with phlegm. Gradually, Lily's coughing became less intense.

"Are you sure that's not from her stomach?" Danny questioned, when the fit ended and they laid her back.

"Get the stethoscope, Danny, and listen to her. Tell me what you hear." Dr. Barton seemed not to hear the question. He pulled Lily forward again so Danny could listen to her lungs.

"Nothing. It's clear." Danny pulled the instrument from his ears and handed it to Dr. Barton in amazement.

"I've never seen anything like it." Dr. Barton shook his head after several minutes of listening in breathless silence to different places on Lily's back. "It's a miracle. God emptied her lungs of the infection and the water it filled them with. There's no other way. That's all from her lungs, Danny. They're clear."

Lily's breathing was quick and clear, but all of her strength had been completely drained. Neither of her parents spoke for the joy they had. Mrs. Wellington quietly knelt and held her daughter's hand. Mr. Wellington sat on the end of the bed, his hand on his wife's shoulders. When the rest of the family were told the good news, the happiness that filled the house was indescribable. Lily would live.

A while later when Dr. Barton returned home, his whole family was surprised.

"Why are you home so early?"

"Didn't you stop at the Wellington's?"

"Lily's not dead, is she?"

Questions flew at him from six different people.

"Whoa…she's alive. God did a miracle about an hour ago," Dr. Barton answered their worried faces.

"Oh, Pa!" Susie wrapped her arms around his neck. "Now I can make it right with her. Pa, God saved me today! I believe and love Him now!" She was bursting with joy.

When he saw the pure and honest peace of a changed heart, he hugged his daughter again, her joy spreading into his soul. "Today is a day of salvation, isn't it?"

~~~

"This feels so good."

"What?" Mrs. Wellington came in with a bowl of soup for her patient's lunch.

"Breathing. I can breathe again—how long was I sick?"

"Almost a week and a half," Mrs. Wellington answered.

"No wonder I feel so weak."

"You basically slept all day yesterday."

Someone knocked on the front door. Olivia opened it and found Susie on the other side.

"Hello, Olivia, is Lily up to seeing visitors? I came to see her."

"Umm, I think so—"

"Well, hello, Susie!" Mrs. Wellington came down the stairs with Lily's empty bowl. Her surprised expression matched Olivia's.

"Hello, Mrs. Wellington, I was wondering if I could see Lily. You see, I've been saved by the Lord Jesus and I came to make things right with her. I hope we can be true friends now."

"Oh, Susie! I'm so happy to hear it! Go on. Go right on up. I think you will be the best medicine for her."

At the gentle knock on the open doorway, Lily's head turned from looking out the window.

"Susie?" She didn't quite trust her eyes, after the illusions she'd had from her fever.

"Hi, Lily," Susie slowly crossed the room to the bed.

"Why are you here?" Lily's face showed questioning pleasure, as she motioned for Susie to sit on the side of the bed.

"For a lot of reasons," Susie spoke as she sat. "God's changed my heart, Lily."

"Really, Susie?" Lily's eyes widened, as she weakly reached for Susie's hand.

"Mm-hm, two days ago—when your fever broke and your lungs cleared. I don't know how I can ask this of you after I've been so awful, but—will you please—can you please forgive me for everything I've done to you? And do you think we could be real friends?"

"Of course!" Lily blinked tears out of her eyes as Susie hugged her. "I've prayed and prayed so long for you, but I'm having a hard time comprehending it's happened! I guess I didn't have as much faith as I should've."

They spent more than an hour talking and sharing. Amidst her weakness, Lily couldn't hear enough of how God had answered her prayers for Susie.

"Jimmy, will you answer the door?" Mrs. Wellington called over her shoulder, as she and Olivia poured a large pot of boiling water into the washtub.

"Yep." Jimmy opened the door with happy enthusiasm.

"Hey, Will…hi, Stephen!" Jimmy was secretly relieved it wasn't a lady on their front porch.

"Hi, Jimmy, is Susie still here?"

"You kiddin'? She and Lily haven't stopped talking for the past two hours."

"Can you run up and tell her we're ready to take her home?"

"Sure, but their goodbye might take as long as their hello." Jimmy ran up the steps, leaving Will and Stephen to laugh at his view of women's conversations.

"Already?" Susie looked at Jimmy.

"It's been almost two hours."

"Oh, my! I've really overstayed my welcome!"

"No, you haven't! You've been wonderful!"

"Oh, Lily, I'm so glad! I'll come and visit soon—with Mama and the girls, too."

"Bye, Susie! Thank you so much for coming."

"I'll see you soon." Susie walked out of the room with Jimmy.

"You were right, Jimmy, the goodbye took as long as the hello," Will teased when they came down. Susie laughed and shook her head as she picked up her shawl, bidding Mrs. Wellington and the girls goodbye.

~~~

Lily watched from the sofa window, which became her daily residence, as May burst in upon the world with new spring growth and warm breezes. Not being able to move around and help with planting the garden or any other work began to wear on her. She felt useless. Danny brought her a pair of crutches, but after less than five "steps" she was exhausted. Her leg was still healing and it would take longer to regain her strength than it did to lose it.

"Ready, Lil? Everybody's waiting." Mr. Wellington came into the girls' bedroom, where Lily sat in front of her dresser.

"Oh!" Lily's arms came down in frustration and she began pulling out pins for the third time.

"Why don't you just tie it back in a ribbon?" her father suggested.

"I've been doing that for the past two weeks. Besides, it's Jane's birthday. I should do something special for it." Lily started over.

"There's not someone out there that you might want to look special for, is there?"

Lily's head spun around to face him in astonishment. "No, Papa!"

"I just thought I might ask. You're not a little girl anymore, Lil, you're a young woman with a heart that has a great capacity to love a man. If there is a certain person you might be starting to have feelings for, we should talk about it." Mr. Wellington sat on the bed as she continued to work with her hair.

"There have been a few that turned my head," Lily admitted. "But they were just girlish fantasies. They were dreams in my imagination, not *real* feelings. I have no serious feelings for anyone—outside of family, that is." She smiled. "I promise I'll come to you, Papa, if it changes." Lily pinned the last few strands and turned her back to him. "Does it look good?"

"Perfect." Mr. Wellington stood as she made her dresser orderly.

"I feel like I'm going to break your arms one of these times," she said, as he picked her up once again and carried her out of the room.

"You won't," Mr. Wellington chuckled lightly.

"Here they come!" Johnny came running in front Mr. Wellington and Lily.

Everyone was there, Pearl and Mark, and Luke and Alice along with the Bartons.

Out in the lovely spring breeze, Lily watched her family members and the Barton siblings with longing. While she was bound to sitting, they were free to run and move as they pleased.

"I will be so glad to see this splint removed," she told Susie. "And that's at least two weeks away Danny says."

"Don't worry, Lil, you'll make it," Danny encouraged, as he passed by to join Will and Stephen in a game of baseball with the others.

"Aren't you going to play, Susie?" Will asked.

"Yes, she is. Go on. I'll be your cheerleader," Lily said, before Susie could respond.

"Are you sure? I don't want to leave you by yourself."

"Oh, don't worry. I will be plenty busy enjoying your new baby brother," Lily grinned with a wink. Just a month before, Caleb Thomas Barton had been born and was adored by all.

Cradling Caleb's newborn form in her arms reminded Lily of the two little sisters she had lost. A small sigh escaped her lips. She didn't realize how much she missed holding little ones. Peter was three and getting more independent by the day. Her nephew Drew was now a year old and Melly Jane was four. Her cousin Lucy was almost two and Pearl was expecting a second baby.

Lily looked up from the little hand that had come to touch the blanket and saw Lucy in front of her. "Do you want to see the baby? Your mama's going to have a baby soon, too. So you're gonna be a big sister."

The small girl nodded and her blonde curls bounced. Lily let her come up into her lap and held Caleb in front of her.

"Lu! Come here, Lucy," Mark called his little girl to him several minutes later.

"Coming." Lucy quickly heeded her father's call. *She's certainly learning obedience well.* Lily mused, continuing to enjoy holding Caleb.

By the end of the day, Lily was completely worn out. Stubbornly, she kept on insisting that she was fine. She couldn't take the thought of going back inside the house and missing everybody. But soon it became impossible to keep her eyes open. Her eyes were so heavy.

"Come on, Lil." Her father found her and didn't give her any choice. "You've had a full day," he said as he picked her up in his arms.

"But I want to stay…it's Jane's birthday…" Lily weakly protested, while her head all too willingly reclined on her father's shoulder as his steady and even gait rocked her to sleep. With strong but gentle arms, Mr. Wellington brought her inside and put her to bed.

Chapter 8

A month afterwards, in the later part of June, Danny removed the splint on Lily's leg. She felt like a bird set free from its cage.

"You should still be careful. Don't jump on it. No hard landings…it's still healing. But it needs to bear some weight in order to heal the right way. So take it easy for the next week or so," Danny cautioned her exuberance.

"Okay, Doctor." She was very ready to do all the things she missed since it broke. Standing on it felt so different. Her leg was stiff and it took several turns about the room to get it to loosen up.

"Oh, Liv! I can walk normally again!" Lily's happiness easily spread to her brothers and sisters.

Even though her leg was still weak, Lily went with Susie to Whisper Creek the next day and followed it all the way through the meadow and down to Willow Pond.

"Susie, you know what the best thing about being down in a valley is?"

"What?"

"It makes the mountains so much more beautiful when you reach the top. Even though it was hard to endure my immobility, God showed me that sometimes the best way to please Him is just be still and wait on Him. He definitely taught me patience."

"I'm so glad it's over. Now we can do all the things we've been wanting to for so long!" Susie jumped into the creek with her bare feet. Lily was about to do the same, but then stopped.

"Well, almost," she grinned, stepping into the water instead.

~~~

"The reason I was so late today was because I had to go see the Mayor of Brockton with Mayor Evans and a few other mayors of the main towns in our district," Mr. Wellington said, as they all sat in the parlor that night.

"Why'd they want you, Papa?" asked Davy.

"Because since I'm the county marshal and the district is in this county, they wanted me to go as a representative of the law as well as the people—"

"Go where?"

"Let Papa finish, Davy," Jane scolded her little brother.

"We have substantial evidence that our representative in Washington D.C. has been doing some dishonest and illegal things lately. So Mayor Evans and the others have asked me to go and approach him about it with a few other officials from across the state. I will be leaving in a few days and I thought I'd take some of you older ones with me."

"Really? Oh, I'd love to go!" Lily was the first one to speak.

"I knew you would, Lil. Do you think Tom would let you go for a couple weeks, Danny?"

"I can ask. Are you going by train?"

"Yes. I hope you can get off because it'd be nice to have you around for the girls when I can't be there."

"I can go, Papa?" Jane was the next to ask.

"Me, too?" Olivia said.

"Well, I can't take all of you. Mama needs some help here with the others. What I'm getting paid for doing this is only going to be enough for three of you to go. It's a little late to start planning tonight, but I'd like to get everything settled tomorrow so we can leave the beginning of next week."

The excitement seemed to infect everybody as they prepared to go to bed. Lily had a strange feeling in the pit of her stomach. Someone had to stay home. And deep inside she felt Someone telling her that she was the one. *But, Lord, I want to go so bad! I'd love to see our nation's capital. Oh, please let me go!* she inwardly begged, getting under the quilt next to Olivia.

The subject was thoroughly discussed the next night at the supper table.

"You've been on a train before, Lily, and you've been all the way to Richmond," Jane pointed out, understanding that Lily would have first choice since she was older. It had already been decided that Olivia and Danny would go. So the question remained between Lily or Jane.

Lily's heart sank. She knew her sister was right and she knew she should stay. "You go, Jane, I'll stay," she forced herself to speak. Even though she longed for it more than anything, Lily couldn't say no. She knew it would be wrong if she insisted on her own way. For the next two days she helped Jane and Olivia pack, trying to hide her disappointment.

"Lil?" Danny came to his sister on the day of departure.

"Yeah?" Lily looked up from the ground and stopped swinging.

"You really wanted to go, didn't you?"

"Mm-hm." Lily didn't meet his eyes.

"You're not mad or grudging, are you?"

Lily met his gaze. "Of course not! Utterly disappointed, yes, but not grudging." She shook her head decidedly. "It was my choice and it was the right thing to do. Jane should go."

"It's good of you to let her. Well, Papa sent me for you. It's time to go."

"Coming," Lily sighed and followed him. It was a strange feeling she had, as if her whole being was struggling to go, but she just couldn't do it. She was held back by her love for her sister and the desire to obey God.

The wagon rolled to a stop at the Brockton Station and Mr. Wellington bought the tickets. Lily thought of when she had first boarded a train three years before, not knowing when she would return. Remembering the excitement of it only intensified her disappointment and desire to go.

"Thank you, Lily." Jane hugged her sister. "I love you."

"I love you, too. Soak it all in, so you can tell me every single detail of what it's like when you get back."

Mr. Wellington and Danny picked up their bags and helped the girls up the steps of the passenger car. The great locomotive's brakes hissed as they were let off. The bell clanged and the whistle sounded. As the station platform was filled with steam, the steam engine chugged forward and the remainder of the family waved farewell.

"Well, Lil, it's just you and me to man the fort while they're gone. Papa and I are so proud of you for letting Jane go," Mrs. Wellington told her eldest daughter softly as they headed home. "I know it was hard for you, which makes it even more of an honorable thing. You've got your papa's wanderlust and love of adventure."

Lily smiled knowingly. "Are we still going to go to the Independence Day picnic?"

"I think so. If our plans don't change."

The long wagon ride to the Brockton Station and back made the boys quite restless. They were loud and bouncy in the wagon all the way.

"Boys, calm down and don't be obnoxious to your sisters," Lily told them. "Girls, don't be aggravating and asking for it either." Her words didn't do a lot of good. When they arrived home, Jimmy, Johnny and Davy ran off in a flash.

"Don't go far. Lunch will be ready soon!" Mrs. Wellington called after them. "Some days I don't know what to do with them." She shook her head. "They have so much energy."

Over lunchtime gray clouds of rain billowed over the sun, making the weather look like the mood Lily was trying to shake off. Not long after, the sky burst open with heavy rain and thunder.

"Can we go outside in the rain, Mama?" Johnny asked.

"No, it's thundering out there. You find something good to do inside."

"Yes'm," he sighed. But he and his brothers seemed to forget the word 'good' and started teasing their sisters.

"No! Davy, stop! Don't!" Sarah's cry from their bedroom soon reached Lily's ears. Lily called for them to stop it and returned to reading her book. The quiet didn't last long. Several more shouts erupted before the twins, Davy and Mickey, came stampeding down the stairs with Sarah and Rachel hot on their heels yelling at them as they went.

"Boys!" Mrs. Wellington came out of the classroom where she had been looking at schoolwork. Coming to her mother's aid, Lily snagged Jimmy by the seat of his pants, but she didn't get a good hold so he pulled loose. Lurching forward and colliding with Davy, there was a loud snap and crack as they landed full force on the piano bench.

"Boys!" Mrs. Wellington cried in dismay. She and Lily helped them up to find the piano seat splintered in two. "Oh! What on earth do you think you were doing?"

"Playing Indians," Johnny answered.

"And aggravating your sisters at the same time," Lily accused. They didn't have an answer to that.

"I told you to find something *good* to do. How many times have I told you *not* to aggravate your sisters?" Mrs. Wellington felt as if her words were bouncing off the walls. "Sarah, Rachel, you know not to keep yelling if the boys don't stop bothering you. You're supposed to come and get me, not chase after them yelling and screaming."

The girls looked at their feet.

"Now through all of this the piano bench is broken…beyond repair I'd say." Mrs. Wellington made a helpless gesture with her hands. "Boys, set the pieces out on the porch. Sarah, please go get the broom for the splinters. Then you can all sit down and read a book."

"What are we going to do now for a bench, Mama?" Lily asked, as the children set about their assigned tasks.

"Maybe tomorrow we can visit the Bartons and ask Stephen and Will to make a new one. We can bring them the pieces to use as a model." Mrs. Wellington sighed.

The boys apologized to their mother and sisters after they'd put the broken bench on the porch. The girls readily followed their lead and then things went a bit smoother.

~~~

The fourth of July was on Thursday. Lily was used to having the kitchen crowded with all the girls making pies the day before. But on Wednesday, it was only her. Mrs. Wellington had decided not to enter. Unable to make one by herself yet, Sarah begged to help Lily and together they enjoyed making a blackberry lemon pie.

"Okay, we'll split it, fifty-fifty. If we win, I get the ribbon and if we lose, you get the blame," Lily joked.

"Oh!" Sarah laughed at her silly sister.

"Don't worry, it'll be the other way around," Lily smiled.

"I'll drive the team, Mama," Johnny offered at breakfast on the morning of the picnic.

"Thank you, sir," she smiled happily.

When they arrived the children nearly fell over one another in their eagerness to get out and go play games.

"Why didn't you put your name down, too?" Sarah looked at the paper on which Lily had filled out the number and name of their entry for the pie contest.

"Because if we win, you get the ribbon and if we lose, I get the blame—fifty-fifty, remember?" Lily winked.

As Sarah ran off to play games, Susie and Beth came running up to Lily breathlessly smiling. "Don't you ever stop moving? First we saw you at your wagon, then you went helping your mama with food and now over here entering a pie! We've been chasing you all around the pasture!" Susie exclaimed.

"Sorry, I have a lot to do." Lily laughed. "Where's Anna?"

"That's partially why we've been hunting you down. She said to meet her at the lemonade table," Beth responded.

Anna was waiting at the lemonade table like she had said. There was a twinkle in her eye and smile on her face that Lily didn't understand. As the four started walking away from the activities and people, Anna told them she was now being courted by a young man.

"Who?" Beth cried. Susie just smiled along with Anna.

"William Bryant. He asked Pa just yesterday."

"Oh, Anna!"

Lily just smiled. The conversation kept flowing and she maintained herself fairly well, but she felt alone, left behind and depressed.

"Lily!" Sarah called from across the field.

"I'll be back." Lily broke into a run toward her sister, glad to have time to collect herself.

"Can you watch Peter for a while?" Sarah anxiously asked. "He's been getting into trouble and the girls' races are going to start."

"Yes, here give him to me." Lily picked Peter up.

"Thanks." Sarah hurried away to where the races were held. Lily slowly followed, not quite ready to rejoin her friends.

"Come on, Buddy, let's go see the race." Lily swung Peter around, all the while wondering why she was feeling so glum. *What's wrong with me? I should be rejoicing with Anna and all I can do is mope and feel miserable! I'm feeling sorry for myself...a pity party...* It hit her then. She had been focusing on herself and what she wanted. *Ever since Papa and the rest left on Friday, I've just felt sorry for myself. Lord, I'm sorry! Help me not to think about myself, but to focus on You and what I can do for others.* Her gloomy cloud of self-pity lifted and happy contentment filled her heart again as she watched the race begin.

"Go, Sarah! Go!" Lily cheered. Her younger sister was in third and gaining. "She did it, Peter! Look! Sarah won!"

"Yeah!" Peter clapped.

"I did it, Lil!" Sarah held out a blue ribbon for her sister to see.

"You were great. Let's get some lemonade to cool off."

They held a small celebration at the lemonade table.

"I can take Peter, now." Sarah put her cup down.

"Well, I'm okay with him. You can go play more games."

"All right."

Lily set Peter down and walked with him to find Susie, Beth and Anna. *Lord, give me joy for Anna.*

"Sorry I took so long. I had to get Peter and I watched Sarah in the girls' race," she apologized when they found the girls.

"Did she win?" Anna asked.

"Yes, so we celebrated with lemonade," Lily replied, noticing with relief and pleasure as they talked that courtship seemed to have left her friend unaffected in the right way.

Susie found Lily alone later. "Lily? Are you all right?"

Lily looked up from Peter. "Yes, I'm fine. Why?"

"Well, I thought you seemed sad when you found out Will was courting Anna."

"To be honest, Susie, I was. But not anymore. I'm happy for both of them and I hope it works out."

"So do I. Do you mind if I ask why you were sad? Or is it too personal?"

"It's not. I was just told at a sensitive time, I guess, because I was still dealing with staying home and not going to Washington D.C. with Papa. I was just feeling sorry for myself and hearing that they were courting pushed me farther into it. Everything is changing and it just made me feel more left behind. But I've made it right with God now and I am happy for them."

"I'm glad. You're a really sweet friend, Lily." Susie put her arm around her friend's shoulders. "The pie contest winners are going to be announced soon, wanna get a good spot?"

"Sure." Lily stood and they walked arm in arm to the dance platform. It wasn't a long wait until everyone was gathered to hear who the winners were. Lily held her breath as the third and second place winners were announced.

"Why are you so excited?"

"Because Sarah helped me make our pie, so I said if we win she gets the ribbon. She's not had much success in the kitchen so I thought I'd help encourage her a little—"

"First place goes to Miss Sarah Wellington for her blackberry lemon pie," Mayor Evans loudly announced.

Lily squealed as she jumped to her feet and clapped. "She did it, Susie!"

Sarah glowed as she walked up to accept the ribbon, after which she ran over and hugged her older sister saying thank you over and over.

"Congratulations you two," Susie smiled.

"Now folks our marshal's not here to say a few words about our history. He is in Washington D.C. clearing up some problem with one of our congressman. But I would like to say a prayer of blessing on our country and plead that she stays loyal to God. Then we'll have the picnic suppers our women have made for us." The mayor's prayer was simple, but full of faith and very meaningful to everyone.

"Your pie was the best, Sarah," Stephen complimented her, when the pies had been cut and served out.

"Thanks. It was really Lily's pie. I just helped and she let me have the ribbon." Sarah shyly gave her sister the praise, glad to have gotten the ribbon.

As dance music began to play, Lily stood by the platform watching partners gather on the wooden boards.

"Do you want to dance with me, Lil?" Jimmy came by her.

"I thought you didn't like dancing." Lily laughed, but followed him to the floor boards.

"It's not too bad now. 'Sides Papa and Danny are gone, so that makes me and Johnny the men of the house. So that means we have to look out for you ladies; you know, drivin' the wagon, doin' the chores and dancing with you."

"Why, thank you, kind sir," Lily smiled widely. Her brothers were certainly turning into gentlemen.

"May I cut in?"

Jimmy nodded somewhat reluctantly and allowed Douglas Collins to dance with Lily. For some reason, he seemed to be paying more compliments to Lily and trying to go out of his way to be chivalrous. She didn't like his attention and had never wanted it. Uttering some excuse about seeing if her mother needed help, she left him right after the song ended.

"Mama, do you need me to take care of Peter?"

"No, I'm doing all right, you just enjoy yourself."

Lily moved on and sat on the edge of the platform by the musicians to watch the dancers go by.

"Hi, Lily," Stephen came around on the outside of the platform.

"Oh, hi, Stephen." Lily turned to face him.

"Will you let me have the next dance?"

"Sure."

"When will the rest of your family get back?" Stephen asked, helping her up.

"Probably not for a week or two. 'Cause Papa's going to ask 'round and see what he can find out first hand before he confronts our representative."

"Pa's sure missed the help Danny gives him with his patients."

"Well, Papa wanted him to go to accompany the girls while he was doing business." Talking about them made Lily's mind wander as they joined in the dancing. She so wanted to know what Olivia, Jane, Danny and Mr. Wellington were doing in D.C.

"You probably miss having them at home?" Stephen's voice broke through her mind.

"What?" Lily brought her mind back to the present.

"I asked if you're missing them."

"Oh, yes. I was just thinking…I can't imagine what Washington D.C. must be like."

"Must be quite a sight," said Stephen.

"Mm-hm…"

Darkness fell and the last ray of sunlight disappeared with a boom as the fireworks began to blast into the air.

"This is my favorite part!" Susie sat down with Lily on the platform's edge.

"I love it, too."

They watched together as more starbursts of color exploded in the sky. When the show was over, Mrs. Wellington began to gather her children to go home.

"Lily, please find Jimmy and Johnny?"

"Yes, Mama." Lily obeyed, but couldn't find them.

"Stephen, have you seen Jimmy and Johnny? We need to leave and I've looked everywhere..."

"You tried under the platform?"

"Mm-hm."

"Out in the field?"

"Mm-hm," Lily's eyebrows raised in question at the comical smile that was forming on Stephen's face.

"Raaoorrr!"

Lily spun around to see her two brothers laughing impishly behind her. They had been skipping from place to place, hiding from her. "James and John Wellington—you blasted sons of thunder! If I was your mother I'd—!" she stomped her foot. "To the wagon both of you."

"Bye, Lily," Stephen fought to keep from laughing.

"Bye," Lily said, following her brothers.

"Were Will and I like that, Mama?" Stephen asked his mother, who had come up next to him.

"No—you were much, much worse." Her eyes sparkled with merriment.

~~~

"Lily!" Mrs. Wellington called out the backdoor.

"Yes?" Lily hopped off the swing under the big oak tree.

"Would you please run an errand for me? You remember Mrs. Larson in Elton, don't you?"

"Mm-hm."

"I know it's a long ride, but would you please take these fabric scraps over to her shop in Elton before she closes up? I was talking to her on Sunday and she mentioned that she has a quilting circle every Friday in her seamstress shop. They've been working on scrap quilts to sell for the Brockton Orphanage at the box social this fall, but they need more pieces. I told her that we had plenty of leftovers and I'd get them to her by Friday. Here it is Thursday and it's totally slipped my mind 'til now." Mrs. Wellington made a gesture of exasperation.

"I'll do it, Mama." Lily took the basket of fabric scraps from her mother.

"I don't exactly remember when she closes. So if she isn't open, just run them over to Mr. Larson at the bank."

"All right, I love you. See you later." Lily stepped down from the porch and went to the barn to saddle Amber. Pulling down the tack, she thought, *Well, it's not every day I get to go take a long ride into town on my own...Maybe this will satisfy my wanderlust.*

Chapter 9

"My rifle done, Bill?" Stephen Bryant walked up to the gunsmith's counter.

"Yes, sir," Bill Jennings bent down to the repaired guns that lay under the counter. Finding the right one, he stood up and handed it to Stephen.

Stephen looked the firearm over. "Beautiful, just beautiful—how much do I owe you?"

"Ten."

Stephen's eyebrows raised. "It was that bad, huh?"

"Well, it needed a whole new firing pin and hammer. The old ones were eroding away with rust."

"Yeah, that's what comes of getting stuck in the rain while you're hunting and there's no shelter for a couple miles. No matter how well you clean and dry it out there's going to be some residue of primer and water—just great for rusty misfires." Stephen shook his head. "Well, I've only got five with me. I'll run over to bank for the rest." He tipped his hat and left.

~~~

Lily frowned in frustration. The sign on Mrs. Larson's seamstress shop read 'CLOSED.' "Come on, Amber." She led her horse across the street. A block down, she tethered Amber to a post and walked up the stone steps of the Elton Bank. A fleeting worry entered her mind, when she saw the blinds being drawn. But the door was still unlocked.

"Hello, Mr. Larson," Lily smiled as she stepped into the bank. Her cheerful smile was immediately erased, when a rough hand clamped around her mouth and a six-gun was pointed at her.

"You lissen to me, Missy, you make one sound and your friend and you are goin' to be hearin' angels sing!" her captor hissed in her ear as she struggled to get free. "You plannin' on makin' any obnoxious sounds?"

Lily shook her head against his strong arm.

"Okay then, get over by that counter and don't do anything stupid 'cause I'll be watchin' you." He shoved Lily forward.

With terrified eyes, Lily looked at Mr. Larson. "Just do as they say, Lily, and you'll be fine."

One robber continued opening and shutting drawers as they emptied them of coin and cash, while the other stood at his watch.

"Sam! A guy's comin'!" he hastily whispered a moment later. "We can take him, he's unarmed."

"No! We already got us too many witnesses to deal with and they'll hear the shots!"

"But we could beat him down," his partner insisted.

Sam peeked through the slit in the window shade. "No, he's too big. He'll make too much of a raucous before we can put him down." Quickly, he went back to the counter. "Over here, Brent! Come on! Just act natural, like we's takin' out a loan. You, too, teller! Right here! And if you or the little lady give a single hint to that feller you'll both have lead twixt your eyes!" Sam threatened.

Lily stood trembling at another teller window. She set the basket on the counter in front of her as if she were waiting. *Lord, save us. Help whoever it is that's coming to figure out what's happening!*

Stephen lightly skipped up the bank steps and into the building.

"Hi, Larson! Oh, hello, Lily," he greeted them, thinking nothing of the two men Mr. Larson was helping.

"Oh, hello, Stephen—ahh, be with you in a minute." Mr. Larson tried his best to act normal under the strain of the circumstances.

"No rush." Stephen leaned his elbows on the counter, totally oblivious to Larson's slight hesitation and nervous twitching. "What's in the basket?" he turned to Lily.

"Oh, Mama sent me with fabric scraps for Mrs. Larson's quilting circle, but her shop was closed, so I brought it here for Mr. Larson to take home with him." Lily tried her best. Forcing a smile, she talked casually, but her eyes spoke the opposite of her lips.

Her seemingly stoic blue eyes made Stephen begin to think. Why was she behaving so strangely? She'd never spoken to him in such a weird way before? Her eyes always mirrored the expression of her face. But now her smile didn't reach them. Had he done something to upset her? Why didn't she just put the basket down for Mr. Larson and leave, instead of standing there like she had nothing to do? Lily never loitered.

He didn't let his curiosity stop the conversation. "Any news from your family yet?"

"Yes, I got a four-page letter from Livy and Jane. Jane does wonders with words. I can practically see Washington D.C."

"Really? Did they mention how your pa's business is doing?" Stephen kept trying to figure out her face. *What is she doing? It's like she's double talking...trying to say something else?* He kept trying to make it out.

"They say its slow progress there with policies, politics and all," Lily continued trying to communicate with her eyes, but was frustrated that he seemed to think this was some funny act she was putting on.

"All right, ahh, gentlemen, if you'll just sign here, I'll tend to this other customer and be back to you in a moment. What can I do for you, Stephen?"

"I'd like to make a deposit." Stephen suddenly changed his mind about making a withdrawal. He tried to make eye contact with Mr. Larson to see if he could find out anything more, but the teller kept his eyes down on what he was doing. Holding out three dollars from the cash he had, Stephen looked at Lily again. *Something is wrong—but what?* He cast a sideways glance at the other two men and everything clicked. *It's not a—oh, boy! They're not customers, it's a hold up.* He calmly signed the deposit slip, tipped his hat with a "Thanks, Larson…" and left. As soon as he was out of sight from the window, Stephen broke into a run towards Jennings' Gunsmith.

"Whew, was that close!" Brent peeked out the window. "He went in the opposite direction of the sheriff's office."

"I still don't trust him. Make sure he doesn't double back," Sam said, resuming the job of emptying the bank of its funds.

Stephen Bryant is so oblivious! How could he be so ignorant? Anyone would have realized something is wrong! Why, Lord? Why didn't You make him understand? Lily helplessly trembled in despair where she stood.

"Bill!" Stephen ran through the store's door. "Get me my rifle and a box of amo will you? And hurry!"

"What's the matter?" Jennings handed him the gun and selected the appropriate ammunition.

"I think the bank's being robbed," Stephen answered, loading cartridges into the magazine.

"Why don't you get the sheriff?"

"That's what I need you to do. I'm sure they watched where I went. When you pass the bank, act like nothing's wrong. Just walk, don't run." He cocked the lever and darted outside. Stephen slowed his steps just before the bank.

"He's back with a gun!" Brent alerted, backing away from the window.

"Don't do anything 'til he gets in here!" Sam franticly ran around to the front of the counter next to Lily.

Knowing he was taking an enormous chance, Stephen entered through the door and acted as if nothing else had crossed his mind but the few dollars left in his pocket. "Hey, Larson, I've got a couple more dollars to deposit. Ended up I didn't need them."

His act was good, but Sam didn't take any chances. As soon as the door clicked shut, he wrapped his large arm around Lily's neck and pinned her arms behind her. Only a small yelp was able to escape Lily's throat. "Okay, Mister, drop the rifle! Or I'll choke the lady."

Stephen's grip on the stock loosened.

Lily struggled against the iron hold of the robber. "Don't! Stephen, don't!" her voice barely reached his ears. Lily tried kicking the heel of her shoe into her captor's foot. Sam only grunted under the pain. Stephen helplessly stood there, held at bay by her words. Brent was holding him at gun point. He slowly began to set the rifle on the counter.

"Don't!" With the last of her might, Lily kicked Sam's shin and forced herself against his arm. The sudden pain was too much for Sam to take. He brutally threw Lily to the floor. She only saw the wooden boards fly up at her face before everything went black.

Stephen took advantage of the momentary distraction and shot at Brent. Sam was also gunned down before he could completely clear leather.

"Lily?" Mr. Larson and Stephen dropped beside her still form, as the sheriff of Elton burst through the door. "Lily? Lily, wake up!" A small rasp answered them as Lily became conscious. "Are you all right?" Gently, they rolled her over.

Lily opened her eyes and blinked several times before she responded. "I think so," she answered, slightly dazed.

"Well, you shot the Bailey brothers, young man," the sheriff turned back from having the bandits hauled out of the bank. "If you'll come with me to the office, I'll give you the bounty that was offered for them."

"Bounty?" Stephen raised his eyebrows in surprise.

"Hun'erd 'n fifty," Sheriff Reid confirmed.

"I'll be there in a minute."

Mr. Larson and Stephen helped Lily up.

"I'm all right," she insisted.

"Would you take her over to the hotel and get her some water or something, Mr. Larson?"

Mr. Larson nodded. Ignoring her dizziness, Lily tried to walk. But after three steps she lost her balance and swayed, almost falling to the floor. Lily was forced to accept their help in crossing the street to the hotel and not until she was seated at a table with a glass of water, did Stephen leave for the sheriff's office.

"The Baileys were quite the smooth thieves. They've slipped through many a bounty hunter's hands," Sheriff Reid told him as he counted the money. Stephen accepted the wad of paper with grateful thanks.

"The thanks is all mine. Those two were an itch I couldn't scratch for the longest time."

"Doing better?" Stephen pulled out a chair to join Mr. Larson and Lily in the hotel diningroom.

She nodded.

"Since you're here, Stephen, I'll get back to the bank and try to fix up everything. Folks are probably worried about their funds." Mr. Larson stood.

"Thanks for your help, Mr. Larson," Lily smiled. "Praise God it's over." She rubbed her forehead after he had gone.

Stephen leaned back. "Oh, before I forget..." he pulled the money out of his pocket and set a third of it in front of her.

"What's that?"

"Yours."

"Oh, no you don't." Lily shoved it back at him. "I didn't have any part of it, and I don't want any part of it either."

Stephen didn't argue, he decided to get it to her some other way. "Okay—feeling ready to ride back?"

"Mm-hm." Lily stood and they walked out of the hotel.

"Oh, my handbag and bonnet," Lily remembered, when they reached the horses. "They're in the bank."

"I'll get them, I have to deposit some of this reward anyway." Stephen quickly mounted the steps and was back outside in a few moments. "I've just got to stop at Jennings and pay him for repairing my rifle." It didn't take long for him to square the deal and they were soon riding along the main road.

"Mama's going to wonder what's taken me so long." Lily dreaded the thought of having to scare her mother with what had happened.

"Well, just tell her the truth."

"I know," Lily sighed. "Wish I didn't have to…well, at least I can tell her I got the adventure I wanted—and it should satisfy my wanderlust—for now at least."

"Wanderlust?"

"Yeah…I was so disappointed not to get go with Papa to Washington D.C. I wanted to see a new place and have some adventure."

"Why didn't you go?"

"'Cause only three of us kids could, and Papa wanted Danny to be there for the girls. Jane really wanted to go, so I stayed home to help Mama. Anyway, I've seen Richmond and I've been on a train before. Jane hasn't seen anything beyond Brockton." Lily shrugged her shoulders.

Stephen smiled, "It was very nice of you to let her go."

"Well, God changed my heart about it. I'm glad she's having a great time."

"Lily's home, Mama!" Jimmy came running out of the house. "Hi, Stephen."

"Hey, Jimmy."

"What're you doing here?"

"Well, let's just say I had to make sure Lily got home all right. She can tell you the rest, bye." Stephen tipped his hat.

"Bye, Stephen, and thank you for everything." Lily handed her brother the reins as Stephen loped away.

"I was beginning to wonder what had happened to you," Mrs. Wellington came out of the front door. "What was Stephen doing here?"

"He rode Lily home," Jimmy answered her before Lily could. Mrs. Wellington gave her daughter an inquiring look.

"Mrs. Larson's shop was closed, so I went to bank to give the basket to Mr. Larson and I walked right into the middle of a robbery."

Mrs. Wellington gasped.

"You got to see a real bank robbery?" Jimmy repeated in gleeful unbelief. "Oh, boy! How'd you get out of it?"

"Can't you guess?" Lily ruffled his hair. "Stephen came a few minutes after me—now I'll tell you the rest as soon as you're done putting Amber in the barn."

Jimmy rushed to do it and Mrs. Wellington walked with Lily to the house. Lily told her mother the rest.

"Thank the Lord he was there," she said, when Lily finished.

"I know."

"So what happened, Lil?" Jimmy pestered when he returned from the barn.

"Go get the others and I'll tell you all together," Lily told him. He was so excited it didn't take him long. Mrs. Wellington smiled as Jimmy, Johnny, Sarah, Davy, Mickey and Rachel grouped around their older sister to hear the story. She stayed in the parlor doorway and listened to Lily retell her experience in such a realistic way.

"How dare he!" Lily stomped her foot. She had just finished the story and was looking into her handbag. Mentioning the part about Stephen offering her part of the bounty had made her suspicious. She was right. Stephen had put fifty dollars in her purse.

"What's wrong?" Mrs. Wellington asked.

"Stephen left the fifty dollars in my purse."

"Don't try to give it back to him, Lil, it wouldn't work and it might offend him. You'd better keep it," Mrs. Wellington advised, knowing what Lily would try to do.

~~~

The next week, a wagon rolled into the Wellington's front yard.

"Who's that I wonder?" Mrs. Wellington straightened her back. It was wash day and she, Sarah and Lily were right in the middle of scrubbing, wringing and drying.

Lily dried her hands on the apron she wore and walked around the house. "Stephen…" She was a little surprised to see him getting down from the wagon.

"Hi, Lily! Will and I finished the piano bench."

"Oh, good! Now we can get rid of the crate we've been using." Lily skipped over to the wagon to see it. "It's beautiful—how much do we owe you?" she asked, as Stephen picked the bench up and brought it into the house.

"Seven-fifty." Stephen told her, setting it down in front of the piano.

"One minute and I'll get it," she said, going to get her mother's handbag.

"Here you go."

"Thanks." Stephen pocketed the money, replaced his hat and walked outside.

Lily followed him out. "Bye, see you on Sunday."

"Ah-ha…oh, have you heard when your pa's going to be back?"

"He says it looks like they'll be on the Monday train—so just four more days."

"All right, well, I'll be seeing you." Stephen spoke to the horses and started down the road. As soon as he was gone, Lily ran back into the house to try out the new piano bench. Her skirt slid easily across the slick and smooth dark finish. It was a nearly perfect replica of the old demolished bench. After just a short little melody, Lily went back to her mother and sister with the laundry.

"'Bout time you're back," Sarah said. "Who was it?"

"Stephen—they finished the piano bench. It's so pretty, Mama. It's perfect."

"Did you pay him?"

"Mm-hm." Lily started pinning a shirt to the clothes line.

Monday's evening train pulled into the Brockton Station with a deafening roar, hiss and squeal. Mrs. Wellington and Lily kept the children close together as passengers began coming out of the cars.

"Michael!" Mrs. Wellington spotted her husband amidst the crowd. "Over here!"

Picking them out, the marshal made his way with Danny and the girls. Their reuniting was filled with hugs and laughter as they went to the wagon.

"And guess what, Papa?" Johnny stood behind his father as the wagon rolled away from the station.

"What?"

"Lily was in a bank robbery!"

"What!" They all looked at Lily.

"What happened?" Jane prodded.

"Well…" Lily told the whole story again. In turn, tales were told to her of Olivia, Jane and Danny's adventures in Washington D.C. They had Lily totally enraptured.

~~~

August brought a good harvest from the garden and many buckets of berries.

"I don't think these bushes have ever produced so much," Sarah said, picking another plump berry and plopping it into her pail.

"Neither do I. Ouch!" Olivia pulled her hand away from the sharp thorn that had poked her fingertip.

"You okay?" Lily's head poked up from the patch where she was picking.

"Yeah. I wish raspberries and blackberries didn't have such thorns."

"I know, but they're worth it."

And they were. A week later, the Wellington ladies were very proud of nineteen quarts of pie filling and jam.

The Fall Harvest Box Social was in late September and Lily was looking forward to helping the orphans in Brockton with the funds their baskets raised.

The schoolyard was filled with people.

"Hi, Susie!" Lily waved.

"Hey, Lily!" Susie ran up to them as Mr. Wellington wrapped the reins around the brake.

Hopping down, Lily went with Susie to put her basket with the others on the table.

"I wonder who'll buy it this time," she mused.

"Probably some very hungry millionaire," Susie teased.

"Oh, come on, be serious!" Lily gave her a playful shove.

"Okay, I'll try," Susie giggled. "Come on, let's go get Caleb."

"He seems to have grown every time I see him," Lily commented when the baby was in Susie's arms.

"Well, he should be growing the way he eats. He'll be a big and healthy man like his daddy," Susie smiled.

"I doubt Aunt Pearl and Uncle Mark will be here. She's still resting from having Mattie."

"Mattie?"

"Yeah, he was born on Tuesday."

"Why don't they just call him Matt?"

"'Cause Uncle Mark thought Matthew was too long to use all the time, but Aunty wouldn't hear of calling him Matt. She can't stand that nickname."

Mayor Evans was not long in starting the bidding. Jane's was first to go. It was several baskets before Susie's went up and it turned out to be Danny who bought it. Lily tried to patiently wait as the auction continued to drag on. She hadn't hid her basket in the middle of them, in fact, she'd put it in the front. The crowd thinned as more and more pairs left.

Finally, Mayor Evans selected hers. It was third to last. Disappointment filled her as she recognized one of the bidding voices. *No, oh, please don't let him win!* The bidding went higher and several dropped out. Douglas Collins was the highest offer. *No, Lord, please!*

"Six," Stephen's voice fell on her ears. Douglas didn't hesitate to over bid him. The amount grew to a nine dollars and twenty-five cents and Stephen held it. Lily suddenly felt different about Douglas winning her basket. *No, Stephen!* she longed to tell him, *It's not worth it! You can't afford that much! It's only a meal!*

For the first time, Douglas hesitated. But then he opened his mouth with the winning bid, "Ten dollars!"

Stephen waved his hand in a gesture of surrender. At least his goal had been achieved, Douglas had spent more than anybody else on a meal and that would go to the Brockton Orphanage.

Lily swallowed hard, as she stepped forward to show that it was her basket. *I will be kind in thought as well as in deed to Douglas. But, Lord, please help me because I can't do it by myself!* Lily prayed as she forced a smile. At the same time, she cringed at the pleased look that crossed Douglas' face.

At first, Douglas tried to lead her over to a more secluded area away from most of the people, but Lily adamantly insisted on sitting right where nearly everyone was. His actions confirmed what she had wondered about since the Independence Day picnic. *I have to tell Papa*, she thought.

After Lily calmly laid out the picnic supper, she invited Douglas to help himself while she went to check with her father about something.

"I'll be back in just a minute." She left him, trying to seem perfectly normal.

"Papa?" Lily gently tapped his shoulder when there was a break in the flow of conversation he was having with Dr. Barton and Stephen about some technical thing.

"Oh, yes, Lily," Mr. Wellington gave her his attention.

"I need you for a minute, can I talk to you?"

"Sure, I'll be back." He nodded to Dr. Barton and followed Lily.

"What's the matter, Lil?" Mr. Wellington sensed her uneasiness.

"Papa, I think Douglas Collins is trying to pursue me," Lily blurted out in plain speech.

"Why do you think that?"

"I've noticed the way he treats me has changed over the past year. I really noticed it at the Independence Day picnic. But he bid ten dollars to win my basket and he looked so pleased that it was mine—too pleased. Then he wanted to go to the side of the school where hardly anybody was. I didn't let him. He's in the back with everybody else, but I couldn't sit down and eat after that. I had to tell you."

"I'm glad you didn't wait, Lil. I'll talk to Douglas when there's a discreet time…" Mr. Wellington tried to decide what to do to protect his daughter yet be discreet. "Did you pack enough for Jimmy and Johnny to have a second meal? They're always still hungry no matter how much they eat. Let's go get them and you can have at least one of them eat with you."

The twins were more than happy to help. They especially liked having some of Lily's blackberry pie. Lily didn't miss the disturbed look in Douglas' eyes. Though he forced himself to be pleasant, Douglas hoped the boys would finish quickly and run off, but those hopes were quickly dashed.

"That was some pie, Lil." Johnny licked his lips.

"Thank you." Lily smiled.

"We'll help you clean up," Jimmy volunteered, "Excuse me, Douglas." He took the young man's plate away.

"That food was so good! I get your first dance, Lil." Johnny helped her up.

"Well, I guess I don't have any choice in the matter." Each of the twins took one of her hands and led her to their wagon to deposit the basket. Lily smiled securely and Douglas just stood watching them in frustration.

The twins claimed Lily's first two dances. Jimmy decided to take the third, but within the first few musical phrases Douglas cut in.

"It's common courtesy to consent when a gentleman cuts in," he informed Jimmy, who hesitated. "Thank you." Only a moment later, his shoulder was tapped.

"It's common courtesy to consent when a gentleman cuts in," Johnny recited back Douglas' own words.

"You already had a dance with your sister," Douglas tried to hide his aggravation.

"I didn't." Danny came to him from the other side. "Come on, Lil. Thanks, boys." Danny took his younger sister away.

Jimmy and Johnny happily ran off to do something else, while Douglas grumbled to himself and went to the sidelines.

"Oh, Danny, I think we'd better step out, I can't dance and giggle at the same time." To no avail, Lily tried to keep from laughing.

"It was pretty funny," Danny chuckled for a minute and then stopped. "Papa told me about Douglas."

Lily became serious. "Until the way he looked when he bought my basket, I didn't really think twice about his attention. But I'm sure of it now, after the way he took Jimmy and Johnny eating with us and then the dance…"

"I know. Papa saw it, you were right. That's why I came so fast, 'cause I knew Douglas wouldn't take anymore from the twins. I could tell by his face. I don't like the way he was trying to sneak behind Pa's back."

"Neither do I. It was so nice to have Jimmy and Johnny there. I felt safe and they're such fun."

"Good, that means they're doing their God-given duty of protection well."

Lily spent the rest of the evening feeling secure. Although Douglas tried to cut in on several dances, she noticed he never tried to with Mr. Wellington.

"He's scared of you, Papa," she told him on a waltz.

"I know. He should be." The marshal gave his daughter a loving smile.

~~~

Mr. Wellington never found a discreet time to talk to Douglas Collins the night of the Box Social, so he decided to seek the young man out and approach him with the subject.

"Is your brother in, Lauren?" he asked at the Collins' lavish home a few days later.

"No, he's in Brockton on business with Father."

"Well, when they get back would tell him I'd like to see him at my office?"

Lauren nodded.

"Thank you, good day."

Late that afternoon, the marshal was preparing to leave when Douglas came through the door.

"You wanted to see me, Marshal?" he asked.

"Yes, I did. Sit down, Douglas." Mr. Wellington motioned to the chair in front of his desk. He sat in the chair behind it and reclined, praying one last time for the right words. "Did you have something you wanted to talk to me about?"

"Ahh...no." Douglas looked quizzical.

"Really? Your actions seem to attest otherwise."

"Actions?" A faint idea of what the marshal was talking about occurred to Douglas, making him nervous.

"Towards my eldest daughter," Mr. Wellington clarified, though he doubted that he needed to, seeing a glimmer of understanding in the young man's eyes.

Douglas didn't respond.

"Don't play with fire, Mr. Collins. I promise you will get burned." Mr. Wellington leaned forward. Douglas' sullen silence caused him to be blunt. "Lily has no desire for your attention and I don't want you seeing her either—at all. It's hands off—unless *I* say differently."

"Why?" Douglas folded his arms in a belligerent way.

"Because, from what I've observed of your character, it is in need of improvement. If your intentions were honorable, you would have come to me first. You lack the mature behavior of a godly man in that area and in some others I've seen. I don't want you giving her your attention. I hope I've made myself clear."

"Perfectly." Douglas gritted his teeth as he stood up.

"Douglas," Mr. Wellington stopped him at the door. "Don't try anything behind my back."

The defiant look in Douglas' eyes as he left worried the marshal. *I don't trust that young man.*

"What'd Mr. Wellington want, Douglas?" Lauren asked, when she saw her brother return.

"Nothing much, just some nonsense about playing with fire," Douglas replied irritably as he walked up the stairs to his room.

Some nonsense… Lauren mused, even more curious.

Three weeks later, Douglas was strolling through Oakville when he spotted the Wellington wagon roll through the street to Perkins' Mercantile. He had shaken off brooding over Mr. Wellington's subdued tongue lashing, but his mind had not changed. Douglas Collins had always been spoiled and given whatever he wanted and now as a young man, he wouldn't settle for anything less than what he desired.

"No, Peter!" Lily swept her little brother away from touching a glassware item. "You know you're not supposed to touch anything. Just look."

"Rachel…" Olivia looked at her five-year-old sister, who was trying to sneak into one of the big glass jars filled with sweets. The small hand slowly retracted.

"Mama?" Lily came to her mother's side.

"Yes, Lil?"

"Do you think we could buy some fabric? I'd like to make a quilt."

"Maybe, why don't you ask Papa. See what he says."

"How much would it cost?" Mr. Wellington inquired after Lily asked him.

"No more than five dollars for a large quilt."

"Okay, go ahead and pick out some fabric, Lil," Mr. Wellington smiled at the joy that lit his daughter's face.

All of the girls were involved in helping Lily choose material for her quilt. The result was a beautiful contrast of soft blue, moss green, pale yellow and white.

"It looks like spring all over again." Jane ran her hand along one of the bolts of fabric.

The bell on the mercantile door jingled as Douglas entered the shop.

"Hello, Douglas, what can I do for you?" Mr. Perkins greeted him.

"Hi, Perkins, I want to see the belts you just got."

"Yes, right over here…" Mr. Perkins led him to another part of the store.

"Here, Jimmy, you and Johnny can each take a crate." Mr. Wellington lifted one of their crates of groceries and handed it to his son. "You got it?"

"Yup." Johnny hefted the crate and Jimmy took the other one.

"Getting to be quite the strong boys, aren't they?" Mrs. Perkins smiled.

"Yes, growing up too fast for my liking. Thank you, Naomi." Mr. Wellington laid down the payment for their purchases.

"Come on, girls," the marshal called his daughters away from the bolts of material.

"Coming, Papa." They followed the rest of their family.

"Happy birthday, Lily," Susie held out a small package to Lily as they met each other after church the next day. "How are you going to celebrate?"

"We're going to a have a picnic by Whisper Creek with Luke, Alice, Uncle Mark and Aunt Pearl. It'll be fun, but I feel like I'm getting old."

"So did I when I turned twenty in August…well, at least we'll get to be old maids together." Susie's sense of fun made her eyes sparkle.

Lily laughed, but countered, "No, we are not old maids." She took Susie's arm.

"I know. But sometimes it does seem that way. Sometimes it feels like that special somebody is taking f-o-r-e-v-e-r…"

"Time to go, Sue," Stephen touched his sister's shoulder.

"Okay. Coming. We're having the Nelsons over. Bye, Lil."

"Bye, Susie, have fun with Anna." Lily waved to Susie with a wink.

Chapter 10

The vibrantly colored leaves began to flutter to the ground as October progressed into November. Lily watched the seasons change as she sewed her quilt.

"I never thought it would take so long," she commented to her mother in the middle of November.

"That's why quilting get-togethers are nice. You can visit with friends and get a lot of work done at the same time." Mrs. Wellington put the last loaf of bread in the oven. "What do you think we should do about Thanksgiving?" She came into the sitting room and joined Lily on the sofa.

"What do you mean? I thought we had the meal all planned out."

"Not dinner—I was thinking more about guests. Luke and Alice are coming and so are Mark and Pearl."

"Isn't that enough?"

"Yes, but Papa and I were talking about inviting the Bartons over. We thought it might be nice to get together with them."

"The Bartons will probably be spending Thanksgiving with the Nelsons since Will and Anna are engaged now," Lily observed.

"Oh—that's true. Well, it won't hurt to ask." Mrs. Wellington shrugged.

Lily's guess ended up to be wrong. The Bartons were not having Thanksgiving dinner with the Nelsons. Mrs. Barton gladly accepted the invitation for her family.

"Luke and Alice are here!" Jimmy announced.

"And the Bartons are right behind them!" Johnny and his twin were eagerly sitting at the window, waiting to announce the arrival of all their guests.

"Be ready to let them in," said Lily, who was up to her elbows dressing the turkey. Mrs. Wellington wiped her hands on her apron to help welcome the arriving guests, while Olivia, Jane and Sarah continued peeling and cutting potatoes.

There was a loud commotion as Luke and Alice came through the door with Melly Jane and Drew. They were closely followed by the Barton family.

"Happy Thanksgiving, Lily." Susie walked into the kitchen after she managed to hang up her shawl. "Is there something I can help with?"

"Hey, Susie, um…" Lily looked around as she paused to think. "I think it's all under control. I just have to finish stuffing this bird and shove him in the oven."

It did not take Lily long to finish her task, ending with a flourishing sprinkle of herbs on the top of the turkey.

"A beautiful culinary touch," Susie commented with a half-teasing smile, as Lily put the large roasting pan in the oven and shut the iron door. They helped the other girls finish what they had to do and then the whole group ran off to play.

"Lily!" Mrs. Wellington called up the stairs a while later. "Lily!"

"I can help you. What is it you need done?" Alice offered.

"Oh, I need some things from the cellar, but I don't want you stumbling down those dark steps with that new little one inside."

"Oh…" Alice tried to brush it off, though she knew her mother-in-law was probably right.

"Lily Eileen!" Mrs. Wellington made one last attempt before mounting the steps.

"Yes, Mama?" Lily came hurrying down the steps understanding her mother's tone. "I'm sorry, we girls were laughing so hard playing charades that I didn't hear you."

"It's all right. Would you go down to the cellar and bring up three jars of beans and then a jar of raspberry preserves for the rolls?"

"Yes'm." Lily picked up the small lantern they used for lighting up the cellar. A few minutes later, she returned with her arms full of glass jars.

"Do you need me to open them, Mama?"

"No, you can just set them on the table. Thank you."

Lily stopped as she was about to dash back to the girls' room. "What happened to all the men?"

"They're discussing some political issue in the schoolroom," Aunt Pearl told her with a small shake of her head.

"You have to show me your quilt," Susie said, later on when they'd finished their game.

"Oh, that's right. It's down in the schoolroom."

Susie and Olivia walked downstairs with Lily while their younger sisters debated on what to do next. Lily quietly opened the door to the schoolroom. The three girls smiled at each other when they saw their brothers and fathers reclining their tall frames on children's school desks and talking candidly about dealings in the U.S. Congress. Quietly, Lily snuck past Mark, who was leaning against one of the bookshelves that flanked the window to the right of the door, and picked up her basket from the bench that rested under the window.

"Wow!" Susie's eyes widened as Lily laid out the blanket on her bed.

"I still have to quilt the layers and then do the binding. But this is pretty much what it's going to look like when I'm done."

"It's so beautiful." Susie gently touched a block of yellow.

"I think it looks like summer." Olivia smoothed out a corner.

"I'm so glad Papa said I could do it," said Lily.

"I should ask Papa if we could afford enough fabric for me to do one." Susie ran her hand along a row, enjoying the feel of the star pattern. "It's so lovely…and it looks just as warm as a down blanket."

"You should ask about doing one."

For a little while longer, they talked of quilts, patterns and fabrics. Then they went to find out what their younger sisters were doing.

"Mama, have you seen the other girls? We can't find them," Susie asked.

"When you were in the schoolroom, they came down all whispers and giggles and went out the back door." Mrs. Barton shrugged her shoulders.

"The barn." Lily snapped her fingers. She, Olivia and Susie grabbed their shawls and went out into the crisp air. They climbed the ladder into the hayloft.

"Okay, we found you," Susie announced to the moving mounds of hay. A burst of laughter came from under the soft straw. They sat down and joined the younger girls in the cushiony pile.

"Why'd you come and hide here?" Lily wanted to know.

"For fun," Jane answered, tossing an armful of straw at her. That did it. A straw fight started. Squeals filled the barn rafters and everyone was breathless when Davy came running into the barn. "Girls! Mama needs you!"

"All right, we're coming." Olivia got up and started down the ladder. Emma, Marie, Sarah, Lily, Jane, Susie and Rachel followed in a parade back to the house.

"What happened to you?" Alice asked, when they came in the door. The girls hadn't been able to completely rid the pieces of straw from their hair.

"A straw fight," Sarah replied. "Jane started it. We had fun!"

The older girls were soon absorbed in the last minute preparations for dinner. Twenty-six people could not sit in the kitchen, so the parents and the young men ate in the parlor, while the girls managed the younger children in the kitchen. During the meal, laughter and conversation reverberated throughout the house, sometimes making it impossible to hear.

"The worst part about Thanksgiving is all the dishes," Jane stated as they began to clear away the empty plates.

"I know, but at least the more people there are eating, the more people there are to help clean up," Lily said, as she scraped a plate and deposited it into the soapy dish water. "Besides, we should be thankful for them as they show that we've eaten well. Many hungry people wouldn't mind doing dishes if they could have a good meal." All the willing hands made light work of the meal cleanup.

"Let's go for a walk while the sun is still up," Olivia suggested as she set down her towel.

By the time they returned it was dark and time for dessert.

As they ate, Mr. Wellington invited everybody to share something that they were thankful for. The circle started with their guests and proceeded with whoever was ready. At some, there were small ripples of laughter, while with others, there were sober nods and murmurs of agreement.

When Stephen's turn came, he cast a quick glance at Lily, who was busy with her nephew, Matthew, as he spoke. "I'm grateful God helped Mr. Larson, Lily and I to get out of a bank robbery unharmed and without anything missing."

Several pairs of eyes were turned to Lily when Danny spoke: "I'm thankful my little sister's alive and the Great Physician healed her when I'd done all I could do."

"What about you, Lil?" the marshal turned to her after there had been a slight pause.

Lily looked up from Mattie's face. "I'm glad Susie and I are the best of friends again."

"What about still being alive?" Luke asked. "You almost touched the pearly gates twice this year."

"That, too. I am thankful to be alive." She smiled at her big brother.

Lily softly smiled when Susie spoke of her salvation. It was something she was so thankful for, too. Many echoed praise to the Lord for the way He had answered prayer.

~~~

Once again, Christmas was highly anticipated. Olivia was especially excited when Mr. Wellington said they could afford to make her a new party dress, since Jane now fit into Olivia's old one. The girls enjoyed a day of shopping in Brockton, where Olivia selected a beautiful deep violet taffeta.

"It's still not as rich as your blue one," Olivia told Lily, when her older sister was saying how she'd be the belle of the ball.

"But yours is just as beautiful, just in a different way—Oh, Liv, it's *so* gorgeous." Lily brushed the smooth and shiny material again. "If I had a mind to, I could be jealous," she teased with a grin.

"Mama, can I get off at the Barton's?" Lily asked as the cutter hissed over the snow. "On Sunday, Susie wanted me to visit sometime this week. I told her I'd ask you…do you think I can, since we're going right by?"

"I s'pose, just be sure to get home before dark," Mrs. Wellington nodded.

Lily watched the frosty white puffs of her breath as she waited for someone to answer her gentle knock. There was no answer. Lily tried once more with a firmer knock. Nothing happened.

"Oh, dear, they must have gone somewhere," she said disappointedly, walking back to the road. "Well, at least I'll get my exercise." Presently however, she heard hoof beats crunching on the snow behind her.

"May I offer you a ride home, Lily?" the rider asked.

Lily turned and discovered Douglas Collins on his proud black horse, Prince. "No, but thank you just the same. I enjoy walking."

"You were calling on the Bartons, I presume?"

She nodded, but hoped he would continue on and leave her. *What business has he to ask where I've been?*

"I am surprised none of them escorted you back," Douglas continued, walking Prince slowly beside her.

"They weren't home." Lily's step quickened. "Now if you'll excuse me, I need to hurry home and help prepare supper."

"Don't you ever get a break from your family and all those little kids?" Douglas' tone held a faint trace of irritation.

"What makes you think I need one? I love them and we enjoy being together." She was greatly perturbed by what he had said.

"Well, don't be angry," Douglas tried to amend her frustration. "It's just that you're always doing things with your family. You never seem to have time to be with someone else."

Lily pursed her lips and hastened on, totally unnerved by him. She was utterly relieved when they came to the T in the road and he was forced to turn a separate way.

Before she went to bed that night, Lily told her parents what had happened.

~~~

"Stephen, what can I do for you?" Mr. Wellington looked up from his work to see the young man come through the door with a little boy in tow.

"I found this young man in back of our place, stealing firewood from the shop. He also managed to swipe a loaf of bread and a jar of preserves from the pantry." The boy looked about eight or nine. His clothes were baggy and worn, and he appeared as if he hadn't had a bath in weeks. "Do you happen to know who he belongs to? I can't get a word out of him."

"Robby Jackson. Lives on the near side of Elton. His father, Gary Jackson, barely scrapes a living as a handyman. Was maimed in the war. Come here, Robby." The marshal motioned for the boy to come, which Robby reluctantly did.

"You know it is wrong to steal," the marshal kindly put his hand on the boy's shoulder.

Robby nodded hesitantly and spilled the story out in tears. "Pa's sick. He's had a fever for days. Mama couldn't find anybody's wash to do an' we needed wood…Jenny an' Sam are hungry and the house is cold…" Robby broke down in sobs. Mr. Wellington held him until he was calm.

"Even if you need something, it is wrong to steal from people."

"I know…but we needed it so bad and there's no money."

"Did you return everything you stole?"

Robby sniffed and nodded.

"Well, maybe you could find a job and earn money while your pa's sick." Mr. Wellington looked up at Stephen. "What do you think?"

Robby looked timidly at Stephen.

"Are you good with an ax, Robby?" Stephen knelt down to bring their faces on the same level.

"Pa was going to teach me how, but…" he shook his head no.

"How about feeding stock?"

"I feed our horse, Rover."

The marshal looked on as the two made an arrangement. He smiled in seeing the man of God Stephen was becoming. His smile widened as Stephen offered his hand in a man-to-man gesture with Robby.

"Thanks, Marshal," Stephen nodded to Mr. Wellington. "Come on, Robby, we've got to make hay while the sun shines." He grinned as they left.

"There ain't no sunshine out taday," the marshal heard Robby reply before the door shut. "And there ain't no hay to make neither."

"Who's this?" Will asked, when he came out to find Stephen and Robby mucking out the stalls and laying down fresh hay.

"Robby Jackson, he came here while you were in the house," Stephen explained the story. "Come on, Rob, we'll get you some supper, then I'll take you home." He led the surprised boy to the house.

Robby shyly ate his supper. Mrs. Barton tried to draw him out, but wasn't very successful. After the meal, Stephen saddled his horse, put Robby in front and let him control Charger.

"There ya are!" Mrs. Jackson exclaimed when she saw her son in the lantern light. "I was plumb worried 'bout you!"

Robby slid down with his cheesecloth bundle of food Mrs. Barton had sent with him.

"I got a job, Mama," Robby proudly told her. "And this is my pay, a loaf of bread and some cheese, too. Oh, and some broth for Pa."

"Ain't that a bit much?" Nel Jackson looked skeptically at Stephen.

"No, Ma'am, you oughta be proud of Robby—he's a hard worker—earned every bit of that." Stephen was keenly aware of their pride about accepting charity.

"He is a good boy. Thank you."

"My pleasure, Ma'am. Be sure you're at our place bright and early in the morning, Robby."

"Oh, yes I will. Bye, Stephen." Robby waved.

~~~

The Wellingtons were a little later than usual to the Evans' annual Christmas Ball. Some dancing had begun.

A while after they arrived, Lily was just standing by a wall watching the others dance gaily, when her mother came up to her.

"Lily, would you please take Peter for me?" Mrs. Wellington held out the three-year-old. "He wants to go and play, but I'd like to visit with some of the other ladies and he's been running me in circles."

"Sure, Mama." Lily took Peter's hand and Mrs. Wellington returned to her conversation.

"What do you want to do, Peter?" she asked, bringing him close to the large tree and setting him down.

"I wanoo to dance wiss me!" he jumped as he spoke.

"Dance with you?"

Peter nodded and held out his arms.

"Okay." Lily picked him up and swirled him around, but stopped after several minutes.

"Ooh, that's good enough."

"More, more..." Peter looked dejected as she put him down.

"You're heavy, Peter," Lily tried to refuse the begging of his blue eyes, but hopelessly gave in. By the middle of the next song, Lily's legs were aching. She noticed that Peter's head had started to droop with the calming music, so she forced herself to keep going. Eventually, he was nestled in her arms fast asleep.

"Do you want me to take him, Lil?" Mr. Wellington asked, seeing the toddler comfortably snuggled on his sister's shoulder.

"I'm all right for now. I'll just go sit down."

Long afterward, Lily timidly interrupted her brother's conversation with Stephen. "Danny, will you feel Peter? He seems too warm, but maybe it's because I've been holding him so long."

Danny gently placed his hand on Peter's forehead. It was feverishly clammy. "Let's take him to Mama. Be back in a minute," he told Stephen as they walked away.

"Oh, dear," Mrs. Wellington sighed when they brought Peter to her.

"Do you want me to come home with you?" Danny asked.

"Well, maybe we should all just go home. Would you girls mind, Lily?" said Mr. Wellington.

"I'd like to stay, but if you think we should all go…"

Jane and Olivia wanted to stay for the sleigh ride as well, so Mr. Wellington consented.

"You stay with the girls, Danny," he directed. "Mama and I will take the rest home."

"Okay," Danny nodded. He and the girls said goodbye to the rest of their family and returned to the ballroom.

"I hope he'll be all right," said Jane.

"I think he will," Danny assured her.

"Where's the rest of your family going?" Susie joined Lily by one of the walls.

"Peter's sick, he came down with a fever."

"Oh, dear." Susie paused for a moment, then hesitantly asked, "Lil, you don't mind if I ask you a personal question, do you?

"Of course not, Susie. We're close friends now, remember?"

"Well, I was just wondering. Are you kind of starting to feel left out?"

"What do you mean?"

"Well, Anna's going to be married in January and now Dick's courting Beth…don't you feel kind of left behind?"

"I don't think so. I haven't really thought about it," Lily answered honestly. "Are you feeling that way?"

"Sort of, but it's probably just because I'm still getting used to it. Beth's only been courting for a week, but it'll probably work out for them. I hope it does."

"Up to a dance with me, Sue?" Stephen asked, walking up to his sister.

"I think I can manage it." Susie grinned. "Talk to you later, Lily."

"Okay." Lily watched them join in with the others; Will and Anna, Danny and Olivia, Dick and Beth...

"May I have this dance?" Douglas asked, as the song's last note was drawn out to a finish. He had quickly noticed and taken advantage of the marshal's absence.

If I refuse, he'll probably just stay with me...but I won't dance with him. Lily reasoned with herself.

"No, thank you, I'm sitting this one out," she sweetly excused herself and left him, hoping he would find someone else. Her hopes were dashed when Douglas came to her with a small cup of punch. With a small smile, Lily accepted it. She sat like a statue as he seated himself next to her and began talking...about himself, the topic that seemed to be his favorite.

"Excuse me for a minute," Danny pulled himself away from a conversation with Stephen Bryant and Darren Evans. Though his ears were still listening to what Darren was saying, Stephen's eyes followed Danny. Threading his way through groups of people across the large ballroom, Danny approached Douglas. Lily's face brightened when she saw her brother.

"Pardon me, Douglas, but I have a slot to fill on Lily's card. So if you'll be so kind as to excuse us…" Danny took Lily's hand and led her away.

"Sorry, Lil, I should've been keeping a better eye on him."

"It's okay. Though you couldn't have come too soon for me."

"Don't worry. I've got my eye on him now."

Towards the end of the dance, Luke cut in.

"How's Alice been feeling?" Lily asked him.

"She's been doing better. It's kind of funny. She didn't have this morning sickness with Drew."

"Maybe it's a girl—Mama says that sometimes women get sick with one gender, but not the other."

After their dance, Lily joined Alice with Luke.

"Do you want me to watch Drew and Melly so you two can have a dance?" she offered.

"We would enjoy that very much." Alice smiled appreciatively, as she passed over Drew and told Melly to stay with "Aunty Lil." Luke swirled his wife away.

"What shall we do?" Lily asked Melly Jane, as out of the corner of her eye she became aware of someone coming towards them. She didn't know who it was, but she didn't want to find out.

"I don' know." Melly shrugged her shoulders in a charming way.

"Why don't we go and sit by the tree and we can watch your papa and mama, and maybe sing or I can tell you a story."

Lily took her niece and nephew over by the tree. As she sat, Lily's flowing blue taffeta skirt billowed into a circle on the polished wood floor, upon which Melly Jane promptly took her place.

"See, there's your mama and papa…" Lily pointed to Luke and Alice.

"Will you tell us a story?" Melly sweetly asked, after watching her parents for a few minutes.

"What story shall I tell you?"

"The Christmas Story, of course."

"Okay, well…a long long time ago, God sent His Son into the world as a little baby…just like your mama's going to have…" Lily continued on, creatively yet accurately retelling the Nativity. She was totally unaware that she had an unseen audience.

Curiously, Stephen had watched as Lily took her niece and nephew by the Christmas tree. Now he listened from the other side of the tree, as Lily recounted Christ's birth in her own words.

When Lily had finished, Melly Jane pointed to one of the shiny red Christmas balls that hung above their heads. "Can I see that?" she asked.

Lily stood and set Drew on the floor so she could pick Melly up. "Isn't it pretty?"

Melly Jane silently gazed at her red reflection on the sphere. A small cry and a glassy clink caused both of them to look down.

"Oh, no, Drew!" Lily quickly put Melly Jane down. Drew had taken hold of one of the boughs in his reach and finding that the pine needles were sharp, let go so fast and knocked one of the ornaments off. Lily picked him up as he softly whimpered. She was glad the silver ball had not broken. "Would you hang the ball back on the tree, Melly?"

Melly Jane did not need prompting. She eagerly picked up the shining ball. While Lily watched her, Drew grabbed at the strip of lace in his aunt's hair.

"Ow…oh, Drew." Lily winced as she tried to release his little fingers.

"Here they are," Alice told Luke. "They were looking at the tree. Thank you, Lily! I think it's time we headed home and put these two—and myself—to bed."

"See you tomorrow." Lily bade her brother and sister-in-law goodnight, then went to get a drink of Christmas punch.

"Would you give me the pleasure of the next dance, Lily?"

Lily turned to face Stephen. "Yes," she smiled, though her eyes rested beyond him for a moment. Stephen glanced behind him as he led her to join the others. He recognized Douglas Collins eyeing him.

"Are you starting to count down the days 'til Will's wedding?"

"He is."

"Where are they going to live?"

"Well, they're going to board in town at Mrs. Ellis's, then in the spring Will and I'll start building their house. He's already bought the land."

"Is Robby Jackson still working for you?"

"Yes, just until his pa is back on his feet."

"Papa told us what happened. It was kind of you to give him a job."

"Well, he needed it. He really enjoys being treated like a man. He's a good worker, earns every bit of what we pay him. He's made a lot of progress in the past week."

"Is he getting schooling?"

"He was going to school up until his pa got sick. But he's learning a lot of important practical things for now."

"That's good."

"All right, folks, it's time for the sleigh ride. I know it's early. But there's a blizzard heading our way, so we best get going if we want to have a good ride before it comes," Charles Peterson announced as soon as the dance ended. Young people crowded into the hall to get their coats and wraps. The front of the sleigh filled rapidly.

"There's room back here, Lily," Stephen told her, seeing she was waiting for Danny to finish helping Olivia and Jane up. Lily looked at Danny.

"Go ahead, this side's full. I'll be there in a minute," he nodded.

Lily accepted Stephen's help into the sleigh. He climbed in and took the place beside her, sprawling himself out more than necessary.

Nervous, Lily commanded her heart to be still, but it didn't seem to do much good. *Not this again, Lord! Help stay my heart on You!* she prayed. She didn't realize that Douglas had been moving towards the spot next to her and that Stephen had intentionally intercepted him. From what he had observed, Stephen felt that Douglas was not welcome to be in Lily's company.

Danny was the last one to board and Stephen moved over, giving him the reserved space he'd made.

"Thanks." Danny helped himself to part of Lily's blanket as the sleigh slid forward.

Chapter 11

Stephen Bryant tossed his boots in a corner and collapsed on his bed. It was over. But somehow he wished it wasn't. A few hours before, Anna and William had been a glowing bride and groom as they glided away in a sleigh. Stephen treasured the powerful hug he and Will had given each other. The bond of brotherhood was unbreakable. They had done everything together; were the best of friends through good times and bad. *I'm overjoyed that Will found the perfect wife, Lord. Anna is just right for him. She's wonderful! It's just that it's so hard to let him go...help me through this, Father...* Stephen sighed as he looked at Will's empty bed. There was a gentle knock on his, never again to be "their," bedroom door.

"You can come in."

The door squeaked slightly as Susie opened it and padded across the floor in her nightgown.

"Hey, Susie..." Stephen tried to get the melancholy out of his voice.

"Don't pretend with me. It's not easy is it?" Susie sat next to her brother.

"No." With a large sigh, Stephen ran a hand through his thick dark hair. They were silent for a little while, each busy with their own thoughts.

"Never thought something could be so wonderful and so awful at the same time," Susie finally spoke.

"Yeah…I guess that's why they call it bittersweet."

"Have you found someone yet?"

Surprised, Stephen turned to fully face his younger sister. "Why do you ask?" he answered her with a question.

"I don't know. I guess a wedding just gets one thinking along those lines."

"I haven't really thought about going that far yet. I'm praying about it…it's kind of soon…"

"But you do have someone in mind." Susie smiled.

"You don't have to read so well between the lines, Sue…Yeah, I've got a girl in mind. I was sorta surprised that Will didn't choose her…but I guess that might be a way of God saying she's the one for me."

"Is it who I'm hoping?" Susie's anticipation eagerly shone in her eyes.

"If we think alike, like I think we do—yes. But don't say anything to anybody. I haven't really talked to Pa and Mama about it."

"I won't—love you. Goodnight!"

"Love you, too, Susie." Stephen hugged her. "Goodnight."

Susie went to the door, then stopped. She turned around to face her brother again. "She'll fall head over heels for you, Stephen Bryant."

"What?" Stephen turned to face her, but Susie was already gone.

~~~

"We've put in a full day of work, Robby. I think we can call it quits," Stephen said as he hung up a saw. "You learn fast. Will will sure be surprised to see how much improvement you've made. Let's see…" he pulled a small leather bag from a drawer. "What'd you earn this week?"

"Well…" Robby looked up. "Five cents a day, I worked five days so…twenty-five cents!"

"You're gettin' too smart, Rob." Stephen playfully pulled the boy's hat over his eyes and took out the change from his leather bag. Robby looked at it with excited eyes. At that moment, he felt like the richest man in the world.

"Thanks!"

"Wait…here's a late Christmas present." Stephen flipped him a nickel. "Buy some candy for Jenny and Sam, too."

"Oh, boy! Thanks, Stephen."

"You're welcome. Now get home before it's dark. You don't want to worry your mama."

"Yessir." Robby Jackson happily ran out of the shop, feeling like a millionaire.

Stephen laughed softly as he watched him go. Robby had helped fill the hole William had left.

When Will and Anna returned from their honeymoon, the Bryant Brothers' Carpentry operated at its normal pace once again. Will was indeed impressed with the progress Robby had made. Both Mr. and Mrs. Jackson couldn't express how proud they were of their son.

~~~

With skates slung over their shoulders, Lily and her sisters tromped through the crusty snow to the Barton home.

"Hello, girls." Mrs. Barton answered Jane's knock.

"Hello, Mrs. Barton, we were wondering if Susie, Emma and Marie could come skating with us?"

"Sure, step in for minute and I'll call them."

Emma and Marie came running down the stairs at their mother's call.

"Where's Susie?" Mrs. Barton asked as they got their coats, mittens and hats.

"I think she's in the shop with Stephen and Will..." Emma pulled on a boot.

Lily hesitated, she was the closest to the door, but she hoped one of the Barton girls would go. None of them moved because they were still getting ready, so she went out and crossed the

Lily—A Legacy of Hope 201

distance to the shop, which was not far from the barn. A soft hammering greeted her ears as she gently opened the door.

"Hi, Lily," Susie greeted with a smile. Her brothers paused their work and said hello.

"Hello," Lily smiled. "We girls are going skating at Willow Pond."

"Oh, fun! I'm coming. I have the most wonderful news! Well, it's really Will and Anna's news, but they said it's okay for me to tell." Susie stepped over a pile of saw dust.

"What is it?"

"I'm an aunt!" Susie could barely contain herself.

"Oh, Susie! That's so exciting!" Lily clasped her hands together before hugging her friend. "Congratulations, Will! That's wonderful! Tell Anna I'm very excited for her!"

"Thank you, I'll do that. Have fun." Will proudly glowed as he picked up another nail and the girls stepped out the door.

"She's the one, Will…" Stephen bounced a chisel in his hand as he set back to work.

His brother needed no explanation. He understood.

The girls talked all the way to the pond. The February weather had been unusually cold. They sat on the flattened reeds and laced up their skates. Since there was a slight dusting of snow on the ice, their skate blades left fun curvy lines as they glided along.

"We should try and write something," said Olivia.

"Like what?" Susie asked.

"Well, I don't know…how about snow? Or ice, or winter?"

The girls' noble attempt at writing 'snow' didn't quite work. The result looked like a tangled mess of yarn.

"Oh, well, we tried anyway," Emma shrugged.

From then on, they tried to do simple stunts. Often the tricks would be a failure and they would break out in hysterical laughter at how comical someone had looked in their attempt. But their fun was brought to an abrupt end when the ice broke out from under Marie. She was unable to stop in time to keep from skating over the spot of ice that they knew to be weak from the flow of Whisper Creek.

"Marie!" Susie cried, hearing the sickening crack. The girls rushed to the hole where Marie was beginning to disappear.

"Help…Susie!" Marie tried to climb back up, but the thin ice kept breaking under her weight. Susie, Lily and Olivia laid on their stomachs to edge closer, while Emma and Jane scrambled to get a branch. Blessedly, there was a dead tree limb that was sturdy enough and Marie was able to be pulled out onto the thick ice.

"Let's get you home." Susie took off her coat and wrapped it around her little sister. "Can you walk?"

"I can try," Marie said through stiff lips. She soon discovered that she was too numb and cold to move very well. So she piggybacked on Susie until her older sister was too tired to carry her anymore, then Olivia took a turn and Emma, too. They hurried as best they could. Lily took her turn when Emma couldn't carry her anymore. Marie continued to get colder.

"Mama!" Some of the girls rushed ahead of Lily and Marie as the house came in sight. Will and Stephen came out of their workshop hearing the girls' cries.

Will relieved Lily of her burden.

In almost no time, Mrs. Barton and Susie had Marie out of her soaking clothes and in a flannel nightgown by the fire.

"Liv, Jane, Sarah," Lily motioned to her sisters that they needed to leave.

"You stay and warm up with some cider first," Mrs. Barton instructed.

Lily tried to refuse, but the doctor's wife was adamant. "You and Olivia should get out of your wet coats for at least a few minutes," she said. Lily gave in and they sat around the fire with Marie. They began talking and laughing again about how ridiculous they had made themselves look.

The guys enjoyed a break from their work and listened to the girls' hysterical laughter over cups of cider as well. It was contagious. They were soon chuckling at their sisters' descriptions. Very thankful for the Lord's protection to Marie, the girls finally left as the sun was spreading an orange glow everywhere.

~~~

"Mama!" Lily came cascading down the stairs on Saturday, after they had returned from town. Olivia and Jane followed in her wake. "Can we go sled—ing?" Lily stopped short to keep from colliding with her father, causing her sisters to bump into her. Just beyond Mr. Wellington, stood Stephen. Lily bit her lip in embarrassment. "Oh, hi, Stephen—Can we go sledding, Mama?" she tried to shake off her mortification.

"Yes, you may," Mrs. Wellington answered.

"Thanks." The girls turned to go get ready.

"Lil, can you come here for a minute?"

"Sure, Papa." Lily followed his motion to the schoolroom.

The marshal met his wife's eyes and gave a knowing look before he joined his daughter and shut the door behind them.

"Would you like some coffee, Stephen?" Mrs. Wellington offered.

"No, thank you, Ma'am," Stephen declined.

"Why don't you go ahead and make yourself comfortable, they won't be too long."

Stephen rotated a kitchen chair around and straddled it. He couldn't get his sister's words out of his mind. *She'll fall head over heels for you... Could she?* he wondered, leaning his elbows on the chair's back.

"What is it, Papa?" Lily asked, noticing her father was unusually sober.

"Sit down, Lil. Don't worry, you haven't done anything wrong." Mr. Wellington smiled. "How do you like Stephen?" he continued.

"Uh-umm..." Lily stammered, unsettled by the question. "I like him a lot—I value his friendship almost like another big brother."

Mr. Wellington sat down on the desk across from her and looked into his daughter's blue eyes. "He wants to be more than a friend to you, Lily...he wants to get to know you better—with marriage in mind..." He let his words sink in before going on. "Stephen's asked my permission to court you."

Surprised, Lily sat in silence. After overcoming infatuations with romance and contentedly giving her future to God, she was now being sought by a young man she hadn't let herself dream of.

"I told him he had my blessing—if you were willing."

At first she couldn't speak, but after a moment, she smiled and said, "I'm willing."

"You didn't expect this did you." Mr. Wellington moved from the desk and knelt in front of her.

"No...not at all..." Lily shook her head and looked at her father's hands that enclosed hers.

"You're not my lil' girl anymore," the marshal's voice was unsteady.

"I'll always be your little girl, Papa." Lily put her arms around his neck and Mr. Wellington held his daughter tightly.

After several moments, he released her and said, "Well, come on, my Lily of the Valley, I don't think we should keep Stephen on edge much longer."

Stephen was on his feet the moment the doorknob turned. He took a deep breath, as Mr. Wellington and Lily walked out hand in hand. Without a doubt in her mind, Mrs. Wellington joined them.

Lily hardly met Stephen's eyes before he looked to Mr. Wellington.

"It's official," Mr. Wellington told him. Stephen's face relaxed into a smile.

Lily smiled in return.

~~~

The Bartons followed the Wellingtons home after church the next day. The sleighs swapped and mixed up passengers. Lily tried to keep her heart still when Stephen climbed into their sleigh with Susie. *Lord, be my guide and let Your will be done*, she prayed, making herself relax and behave as she normally did.

There was a rush in the entry hall as the women and children went into the house and the men took care of the animals.

"My, it's been a cold February!" Mrs. Barton rubbed her hands together after depositing her cloak and bonnet on a hook.

"Hasn't it, though?" Mrs. Wellington agreed, heading into the kitchen. "You children find something to do inside for a while, then maybe you can go outside later."

So many hands were helping with dinner that Lily and Susie left the kitchen because they were in the way more than anything.

"Have you heard about the bazaar that Brockton is planning in late April?" Susie questioned.

"Mm-m." Lily shook her head. "That's an awful long ways away—well, I s'pose not really, since it is late February." Lily pulled her feet up under her and leaned on the arm of the sofa.

"Papa had to see the mayor's wife and that's how we found out. It's supposed to raise funds for the orphanage to pay for roof repair, new beds and some other things that they don't have money for. Mama was thinking of setting up a quilting booth or maybe knitting and crocheting."

"Does all of the money go to the orphanage?"

"Most of it, I think—" Susie stopped, as their fathers and older brothers came in the door.

"How long 'til dinner?" Danny asked, wiping off his boots.

"Not too long," Lily told him.

"Feel like checkers, Stephen?"

"Sure." Stephen sat in one of the chairs that flanked the sofa. Danny seated himself on the sofa's end that was next to him and laid out the checkerboard and pieces on the small table between them. For a few minutes, their sisters looked on in mild interest, but they soon returned to the topic of the Brockton Bazaar.

"No!" Danny's cry of defeat interrupted them a while later. "That's the second time in a row! How's that happen?"

"That's a good question. Never thought I'd whip you like that. We're usually going neck and neck." Stephen began reorganizing his pieces.

"Now you know how I feel when you beat me, Danny," Lily jibed her brother.

"Why don't you play him?"

"Me? If he beat you, he'll kill me for sure," Lily declined.

"Oh, come on—you're almost as good as me."

"Almost—" Lily weakened in her decision.

"Oh, go play, Lily," Susie encouraged.

"I'll be easy on you," said Stephen.

"That'd be cheating—besides, I want to win by myself. If you let me win, it wouldn't really be winning. I'd rather lose in that case." Giving in, Lily took Danny's seat. She was given the first move. In the middle of the game, Stephen smiled as he didn't go easy on her and double jumped her pieces. Biting her lip, Lily groaned. For several minutes, she berated herself and scrutinized the board for her next move.

"Oh! Oh, oh!" Lily flapped her hands in her excitement, something she often did when she was joyfully surprised. Victoriously, she performed a double jump and "king-ed" her piece, the first one of the game.

"What?" Stephen almost jumped out of his chair.

"Your move." Lily couldn't conceal her triumph.

Dinner was announced a few turns later and they had to pause. When the game commenced afterward, Stephen won. Lily hadn't realized how competitive she'd become.

"That was an awfully close game. For a while I thought for sure you had me beat, especially after that double jump," Stephen admitted.

Lily half smiled. "I gave up on winning checkers a long time ago. I only got good enough to give Danny a run for his money. But then he got as good as Papa and that was the end of the fun."

"Are you done with the game yet?" Emma and the other girls came down the stairs.

"Yes, and I lost." Lily stood up.

"You should teach her your tricks, Stephen," Marie told her brother.

"She doesn't need any teaching. She double jumped me and got a king all in one go."

"But she still lost," Marie pointed out.

"Uh-huh…" Stephen smiled.

"Since they're done, can we go skating now, Papa?" Johnny turned to Mr. Wellington.

"All right, let's go."

Even Mrs. Wellington and Mrs. Barton ventured out for a little while with Caleb and Peter.

"Livy and I have to show you this new trick we came up with. It's so much fun to do," Lily told Susie, as they marched through the crusty snow.

The girls hurried to put on their skates to perform their stunt. Olivia and Lily skated towards each other from opposite sides of the pond, then linked their arms and spun around pulling themselves closer together. It turned out to be a failure. They lost their grip on each other and sped away in different directions. Losing her balance, Lily fell and slid to a halt just before the snow bank. Olivia was more fortunate and careened to a soft landing in snow-covered reeds.

"That was the best one yet!" Jimmy doubled over laughing with the rest of the girls' audience. It was quite the scene, one sister was sprawled out on the ice and the other buried in a snow bank.

"Oh, ha-ha, very funny!" Olivia stood and brushed herself off. Stiffly, Lily got on her knees and stood on her blades again.

"Let's try it again, Liv, and this time don't let go."

"You're telling me." Olivia glided to her side of the pond.

Their second try went like it was supposed to. Several similar spills occurred when the Barton girls tried to do it.

"It's not as easy as it looks. It's hard to keep your balance when you're spinning around so fast," Emma said after her failure with Jane.

"Try going slower," Stephen suggested.

Lily—A Legacy of Hope 211

Following his advice made it go much better for the girls and they even finished with a graceful flare.

"You two do better than Livy and I ever have," Lily told them, as she and Stephen passed by the girls while they skated around the pond. A few minutes later, a snowball hit Lily squarely on the back. "Who did that?" she demanded, glimpsing a mischievous Davy speeding away from sight. "You asked for it, Davy boy." Lily stopped at the bank, scooped up a handful of snow and packed it into a ball. Hurling it, she miss-aimed and hit Johnny.

"Hey!" Her younger brother turned around with a slight scowl that quickly melted into a teasing look.

"Sorry, Johnny," Lily rambled quickly. "I was trying to hit Davy and you know what a terrible throw I am—Oh, no!" She held up her hands defensively and ducked to avoid the ball of snow Johnny chucked at her. The thirteen-year-old's well-aimed missile missed its side-stepping target and hit her suitor instead. Stephen was already well stocked in ammunition. He smoothly hit Johnny back and pitched one at Davy. Snow was flying through the air and hitting miscellaneous people. By the time it was done, most of them were all white.

"My hair is going to be so wet when we get back, and it's all falling out." Lily tried to comb out the partially melted snow from her hair. But her attempts only made things worse. The warmth of her head had melted the snow just enough to make it into ice clumps that couldn't be combed out.

"That's the one thing about snowball fights: no matter how much snow I throw, I get covered by twice as much and I end up a mess," Susie sympathized as they unlaced their skates.

The Bartons stayed long enough to have some hot cider and warm up. But they took their leave when darkness fell.

News of the Brockton Bazaar spread rapidly and the date was set for Friday, May first. The Barton girls were planning a booth, and the Wellington girls donated their time to help and added some things to the inventory. The families often spent their Sunday afternoons together.

Both Stephen and Lily enjoyed spending much time together. Lily found her hopes and dreams fulfilled, and Stephen was not disappointed in what he had unwittingly set his heart on.

~~~

Green shoots of living plants broke through the soft brown earth in mid-April. The wonderful sprouting of spring life was accentuated with the news of Luke and Alice's new baby girl, Isabella Alice.

Once again, garden preparations were made. Early in the last week of April, they turned the soil and sowed.

"Are you sure we shouldn't shrink the garden down again?" Jane leaned on her hoe. They had never returned the garden plot to its original size after getting through the tough year of house rebuilding.

"It's not really worth it. We'd have to transplant some grass so we wouldn't have mud and it's nice to have a bigger harvest; it gives us a more substantial winter supply," Mrs. Wellington answered, busily hacking away at a dirt clod.

It was late in the afternoon when the last seed was covered and buckets were hauled from the well to moisten the ground.

"That does it." Lily wiped her forearm across her forehead, leaving a dark streak of mud across it. "What are you laughing at?" she questioned, when several of her siblings giggled.

"You look like an Indian, with dirt all over your face," Johnny told her.

"Oh, dear…" Lily rubbed her cheek, only smearing the mud more. "Well, that's what happens when you work in the dirt all day." She picked up a hoe and bucket, then walked toward the barn.

"I almost feel like I need a whole bath," Olivia sputtered through the water that she splashed on her face and arms. "It'd be nice if it were warm enough to go for a swim in the pond."

"Yeah," Lily agreed, as she crossed over to the pump to get her own bucket of wash water. She didn't hear an approaching horse above the noise of working the pump handle and the resulting water flow.

"Hi, Lily." Stephen's greeting brought her head up.

"Oh! Hi—Stephen…" Overly conscious of her appearance, Lily managed a sheepish smile, making her teeth look even more white against her muddy face.

"Hello, Stephen." Mrs. Wellington stepped out of the garden. Lily relaxed as Stephen's attention was diverted.

Quickly, Lily hauled her bucket to the wash stand in back of the house. Wasting no time, she began splashing it on her arms and face. It took a bit of scrubbing to get the dirt from under her nails. Amidst the sloshing of water as she washed, Lily was able to hear her mother and Stephen's conversation.

"I was headin' into town and Mama 'n the girls asked me to return this." He extended a basket which held unused material scraps.

"Thank you!" Mrs. Wellington took the basket.

"And they told me to ask if some of the girls could come early with us and set up the booth on Friday."

"Hey, watch it! You're getting me wetter than I already am!" Jane cried, distracting Lily from listening. In throwing the water out of her bucket, Lily had accidentally been splashing her younger sister.

"Sorry." Lily moved over and threw the water up more than out. She enjoyed watching the large droplets glistening in the lowering sunlight before they plummeted down with a thud on the ground.

"Why don't you just dump the whole bucket all at once?" Stephen asked from behind her with his horse tagging along.

Lily whirled around, sloppily sloshing the handful she had been just about to throw. "C-'cause it's more fun to do it slowly," Lily answered, trying to shake off the embarrassment she felt. "Then I can enjoy the water droplets sparkle in the sunshine—I really like them…" she honestly finished, biting her bottom lip and wishing she could hide because she felt so foolish.

"Lily, Mrs. Barton and the girls want you, Livy, Jane and Sarah to go early to the bazaar with them to set up their booth," Mrs. Wellington told her. "I told Stephen that would work out fine, if you girls want to—though I doubt I need to ask." She smiled.

"That'd be great!" Jane agreed with excitement.

"Yeah, I think that would be fun." Lily nodded.

"We'll probably be by about noon," Stephen said as he brought the reins back over his stallion's neck.

"That'll be fine," Mrs. Wellington responded. "Say hello to your family for us."

"I will, bye." Stephen remounted Charger. "Bye, Lily. Don't worry, I still enjoy splashing in mud and water, too." He winked. "I'll see you all on Friday."

"Bye." Lily waved as he rode off, wondering if his remark about splashing was gentle teasing or meant to ease her embarrassment.

Chapter 12

The day of the Brockton Bazaar was bright and sunny like everyone had hoped. The Bartons arranged to pick up Lily, Olivia and Jane a little after noon to help with the girls' quilting booth.

"Have you seen my white hair ribbon, Liv?" Lily asked, rummaging through their accessories drawer.

"I saw it on your dresser yesterday, when you laid everything out," Olivia replied, carefully sliding her dress over her hair.

"Found it. Must have gotten knocked down." Lily stooped to pick up the silk accessory that lay on the floor between her dresser and the wall. "How do I look?" She stood and spun around after the ribbon was tied in place. The flounce on the hem of her red gingham dress ruffled with the motion. Short sleeves trimmed with eyelets puffed slightly and suited the oval neck trimmed with the same eyelet lace.

"Like a queen, but you forgot your locket," Jane responded. "Will you get this last piece of hair for me? I can't see where it needs to go."

"Mm-hm." Lily clasped her silver locket around her neck and reached out to finish her sister's hair.

"They're just pulling into the yard, girls, you'd best hurry," Danny said, as he passed by their door and went down the stairs. The sisters grabbed their handbags and rushed down the stairs.

"Bye, Mama, see you later," Lily called as she went out the door.

"Good morning, girls," Mrs. Barton smiled as Stephen helped them into the wagon.

Several booths were already in order when they reached the town green.

"It almost looks like a circus," Susie commented as people bustled about.

"Really? We've never been to a circus." Olivia stepped off the wagon.

"We only went once…a long time ago, when we lived in Ralton," Emma responded.

"It's not that much of a sight," Stephen said. "Too many people pushing and shoving, venders shouting over each other to get more business. Pickpockets everywhere and the sights aren't worth the money you lose seeing them. The best part was the acrobats. We saw them perform once."

"Sounds exciting," Lily commented.

Stephen chuckled, "Depends on what kind of excitement you're looking for."

It was mid-afternoon when people were arriving to browse the booths.

"Let's go see what other booths there are!" Emma grabbed Jane's hand. Their sisters and Stephen followed them. There were quite a variety of booths to be explored. Mrs. Harris and her sister, Sally Tern, had a whole stand filled with preserves of various types. There were several game booths, including one with target shooting. Lily couldn't resist stopping there.

"How much for a round of five?" she asked the vender.

"A nickel." The young man pulled his feet off the shelf under the counter and stood up.

"What are you doing, Lil?" Olivia asked.

"I'm gonna shoot off a few rounds." Lily accepted the rifle and five cartridges in exchange for the nickel she dropped into the vender's hand.

"Your pa teach you to shoot or did Danny?" Stephen asked.

"My father, of course. Him being the marshal, he's made certain we girls know how to use guns. Jane and Sarah are learning now, too." Lily easily slid the cartridges into the magazine and pulled the gun's stock snugly to her shoulder. She brought her sights in on the tin can, squeezed the trigger and missed.

"Ooh!" Lily winced and quickly cocked the lever again. This time she didn't miss. The tin can gave a twang of complaint as the bullet sent it whirling off the post. The following three shots had the same result.

"Your pa taught you well," Stephen smiled.

"Thank you." Mr. Wellington accepted the compliment for himself.

"You're here!" Lily turned around with her other surprised companions.

"Yes, I am. The twins had to get going on their surprise booth."

"Those weasels…they've been so mysterious about it for a whole month and won't let on to what they're doing," Lily informed Stephen, before turning to her father. "Did you see? I hit four out of five."

"I only just saw the last one. Good job. Here's a round for you, Liv." He handed his second eldest daughter a nickel. Excitedly, Olivia hit four of the five cans as well.

"Should we do a match, Liv?" Lily asked, seeing her sister's score.

"Okay, you take two and I take two, then the winner gets the last shot."

"All right."

Olivia hit her two cans without a glitch. On Lily's second shot, there was only a slight tink as the bullet grazed the can's side.

"Missed," Olivia said triumphantly.

"Doesn't grazing it count?"

"Nope, sorry, you have to make the can move," the vender told her.

"Oh, that's not fair. I was so close!"

"Great aim, Lil," Stephen said, as Olivia took her victory shot. "I never knew anybody who could graze the side of their target on purpose."

"Oh, thanks," Lily groaned.

"Who won the match?" Mrs. Barton asked, when the girls and Stephen returned to the booth. "Your papa said you were having a shoot out."

"Olivia won—I only grazed the can on my last shot," Lily told her.

"Has anyone bought a quilt or something yet?" Susie asked her mother.

"Mrs. Thompson came by and bought two towels, but she's been our only customer so far."

"Do you want me to mind it for a while, so you and Papa can look around?" Emma offered.

"I'd like that. Thank you, Em." Mrs. Barton took her husband's arm and they strolled away.

"Hey, girls!" Marylou Farns came up to her friends.

"Oh, hi, Marylou!"

"Is Beth here?" Lily asked.

"Mm-hm..." There was a certain sparkle in Marylou's eyes that made Lily wonder. Marylou soon went off to other exciting things; she was like a buzzing bee, never stopping anywhere for long.

"Uh-oh, I know what that means," Susie grinned.

"What?" Stephen looked at his sister, who was exchanging looks with Lily.

"I think Dick and Beth have some news," Lily answered for her friend.

The girls were right. Later when Dick and Beth met them by a ring-toss stand, there was a shining ring of gold on Beth's finger and a glow on her cheeks, as she told her friends that they were engaged to be married the second day of June.

"Wow, that's soon," said Lily.

"Well, we don't really need to wait. We found a house outside of Charlettedale. All there is to do is make the wedding arrangements." Beth smiled. "God has been really good to us."

"Where's Stephen?" Dick asked.

"Oh, Will stole him away. My best guess would be that they're having a shooting match at the shooting booth," Lily informed him.

"You're probably right. I wouldn't be surprised. See you around."

"They make a very nice pair," Susie remarked, watching the couple stroll away.

"Yes, they do. Come on, let's go see the pavilion."

All the booths were grouped around a large, white-washed pavilion that was on the town green of Brockton. Here were centered the main activities of performances by school children and a small band that provided music. Pink and blue strips of crepe paper had been hung around the structure's eight sides and white rosettes graced each corner.

"They did a nice job decorating," said Susie. "Blue and pink are nice for the boys and girls in the orphanage."

"It is cute—oh, look, they're going to do something." Lily pointed as several children were grouping in front of the band.

"There's Robby!" Susie pointed and waved to the boy who often worked for her brothers. He smiled back just as their song began. People eagerly applauded when they finished singing "All Creatures of Our God and King." With beaming faces, the children took their bows.

"They sing well," Lily remarked after they had gone.

"They do," Susie agreed as they turned away. "What shall we do next?"

"Um...I don't know." Lily shrugged. "We could go back to your booth, I s'pose."

They meandered back having no better idea. Danny, Anna, Will and Stephen were there talking with Dr. and Mrs. Barton.

"Did you have a shoot out?" Susie asked her oldest brother.

"Oh, yes."

"Who won?" Lily questioned, after giving Anna a hug hello.

"Stephen. Looks like you and I are in the same boat, Lily, our younger siblings can out-shoot us." Will grinned at Stephen.

"Hey, Johnny and Jimmy said they're ready for you to see their surprise now." Danny came up and took his sister's arm.

"Yay! Finally…"

Stephen curiously followed, as Danny threaded through the crowd and stopped in front of a booth that had a tank of water with someone sitting above it in a clown's suit.

"Three cents fer three balls." Eric Nelson held out a few baseballs. He, Frank and the twins were in charge of the booth.

"Where's Johnny, since you two were all in cahoots over this?" Lily asked Jimmy, as she laid down the pennies and got her three balls.

"Right here, Lily." The clown waved.

"Johnny?"

"Yup. Since you were all head up about not getting in on our secret, you get to be the first to dunk me."

"Dunk you? How?"

"Just hit the target at the end of my bench."

"You know I'm a terrible throw! I might hit you!"

"Ahh, come on, you can do it."

"Go ahead, Lil," Stephen and Danny prompted.

"Here goes." Lily picked up a ball and threw it. She just barely missed hitting her brother. "Oops, sorry!"

"That's okay. Keep throwin'."

Her second ball smacked the target with a hard crack and Johnny fell into the water with a splash.

Johnny was just barely starting to sit down on the bench again when Lily pitched the last ball. With a cry of surprise, Johnny went down again.

"Hey!" he sputtered to the surface again as everyone burst out laughing.

"You wanted me to get you wet!"

Her younger brother laughed. "Don't let her have any more balls, Eric."

"You'd better get used to the water. There's a whole line of people wanting to dunk you now," Frank grinned.

"Bye, guys!" Lily waved as they walked away. "Danny, where are Mama and Papa?"

"Taking the little kids around to see everything—they even got each of them a candied apple."

"Oh, boy! What a sticky mess we'll have when they're done."

The shadows lengthened as the day grew late. The paper lanterns that decked the booths and pavilion were lit. Dancing on the grassy area began.

"First dance is mine, Lil," Mr. Wellington came up to his daughter.

"Of course, Papa. You can have all of them if you want," Lily responded with a smile.

"That'd be fine with me, but unfortunately, I can't dance with all my daughters at once and I have to share you with a certain someone."

"What's on your shirt?" she asked, looking at his shoulder where she almost put her hand.

"It's called caramel from a candied apple that your youngest brother ate."

"Oh…" Lily laughed.

When the song was done, the marshal passed his daughter on to Danny.

"Ready for this, Lil?" he asked as they joined a square dance.

Because it was still early in the evening, the musicians set an incredibly fast pace.

"Oh, my!" Lily wheezed slightly when they were done and sat on the edge of the pavilion. Stephen joined them.

"That square dance too much for you?" he asked, a bit out of breath himself.

"Gettin' there."

"Susie and I barely made it through."

"Danny?" Jane came up to them. "Will you dance with me?" she asked. "It's the Virginia Reel, my favorite."

"Of course, come on." Danny took his sister's hand.

"Feel up to dancing with me?" Stephen asked, when the music stopped once again.

"Sure." Slipping off the pavilion's edge, she took her place on the ladies' side for a line dance. Charlie Peterson's voice rang out rhythmically as he called out the riddles of the dance.

"I'm always amazed at how fast he can rattle those things off," Lily said, as they met in the middle and then stepped back.

"Most of them are tongue twisters, too," Stephen agreed when they came together again.

As Lily stepped back, something caught her foot and she fell flat on her back, brushing against someone in the process.

"Oh! I'm so sorry!" Douglas Collins apologized, kneeling down and extending a hand.

Everyone around stopped and looked. Some asked if she was hurt.

"I'm fine." Lily slowly got up. She was so embarrassed—she didn't know why or how it had happened.

"You sure you're all right?" Mr. Wellington asked, stepping past and in front of Douglas Collins.

"I don't know...I-I tripped and fell backwards—but I'm okay." Lily felt her face flushing red from frustration and embarrassment. She hoped no one could see it in the dim light. When everyone returned to dancing, she relaxed and tried to regain her composure.

"I'm sorry, Stephen. I guess my feet got tangled," she apologized.

"Don't worry about it. Come on, I'll get you a drink." For now Stephen decided not to tell her that he had seen what had caused her fall and that it wasn't her own clumsiness.

The crowds didn't begin to thin until after the stars had appeared.

"Do you want to stay for the hay ride, Lil?" Danny asked.

"Sure, are Mama and Papa leaving now?" Lily understood the question's implication.

"Yeah, they're taking Peter, Mickey, Rachel and Davy home. Jimmy, Johnny and the girls are going to stay with us."

Not long after that, Charlie Peterson pulled his large hay wagon into the dance area to pick up his passengers. Begging to drive the wagon, the twins flanked Peterson on the wagon seat.

Susie and Lily climbed aboard the wagon and plopped into the hay. Their brothers joined them along with Beth and Dick. Even Will and Anna hopped on, too.

"This everybody? Last call!" Peterson shouted. After waiting a little bit, he handed Jimmy the reins and told him to start driving. "Ain't every day I get capable assistants to drive for me. You get the next leg, Johnny." With that said, he broke into a song and everyone else followed.

Some of the girls started singing "Aura Lee" when the first song was done. Everyone else joined them by the second verse, until Charlie Peterson piped up.

Lily—A Legacy of Hope

"You guys are puttin' me to sleep...you'd better pick a livelier song."

Susie responded with "Turkey in the Straw."

Their entire ride was filled with songs and laughter. Lily's sides ached from laughing at all the bantering of Stephen, Will and Danny. It was a while before the wagon made it back to Oakville. When they reached the drop off point for the Wellington home, Stephen quickly got down and assisted Lily off the wagon.

"Thank you," she smiled.

"My pleasure..." Stephen smiled back. "See you on Sunday."

~~~

The evening sun set red below the town of Lyndale, as two weary travelers rode through the main street and stopped at the saloon. They were quite opposite in stature. While one was average height and thick set, the other was tall and wiry.

"Is this worth it, Brett?" lanky Arnold Setters wearily asked as they walked through the swinging doors. "We've been riding for weeks and no one's heard of 'im."

"We'll find him." Brett Whitney sat at an empty corner table. "It's taken us four years to get back on our feet, and it was all 'cause o' him, too. He's gonna pay for what he's done. Why? Are you getting second thoughts?"

"Kinda, Brett. Sure we know he's in West Virginia, but there's a lot of places he could be—'specially within those hills." Arnold paused as they were served full glasses of whiskey.

"Well, back out now or never. Thought you wanted to get even as much as I did. He needs a good whippin'."

"I do wanna get even, Brett, bad. Guess I'm just saddle sore. Think we could get us a room for the night?"

"Yeah." Brett looked around the bar room. "This place shouldn't cost too much. We can sleep like kings tonight and go over the town tomorrow."

The two ex-Confederates didn't sleep like kings as Brett had predicted. They couldn't spare the extra money to get a second room, so they shared the one bed in the room they rented. It was barely long enough for Arnold and barely wide enough for both he and Brett to fit sleeping on their sides. Eventually, Arnold moved to the floor.

Around noon, they began inquiring in different shops. At most, they were disappointed.

"We're lookin' fer a guy by the name of Stephen Bryant. Ever heard of him?" Brett asked over the clang of Hadley Jones' blacksmith hammer.

Hadley's metal beating stopped. "Stephen Bryant?" he repeated, taking in the appearances of the two questioners. "Don't know him. You heard of him, Ben?"

"Uh, sounds familiar..." Ben saw a faint, but very familiar smoldering of hate in the one's eyes. Hesitantly, Ben tried to think. "Can't rightly recall, though...had something to do with a bad event in my life..."

"Do you know where he is?" Arnold asked, keeping his excitement masked.

"No, I can't remember where or what it was that happened...it's all foggy, but he sounds familiar...can't place 'im. Sorry, fellas, but I don't know." Ben shrugged and continued hammering as Brett and Arnold walked away.

"So close!" Brett pounded his fist into the other hand.

"Well, we're in the area, 'cause he heard of him." Arnold tried to look on the bright side.

~~~

"I'm home, Emily," Ben called as he came through the door of their new home. Soon after they'd married, Ben and Emily had sold the boarding house and bought a small home on the outskirts of Lyndale. Emily had thrived on keeping house for only one man and not several people.

"Hello, Dear." Emily came from the kitchen with their baby daughter, Amelia, in her arms and greeted him with a kiss.

"How are you and how's my little girl?" Ben gently settled Amelia in his arms. Her small frame looked even more tiny in her father's strong arms.

"She's just fine. And my morning sickness wasn't as bad today. How was your day?"

"Ahh, fine…funny thing happened, though," Ben said as he followed her back to the kitchen. "A couple men stopped by the shop and asked about a man named Stephen Bryant."

"What's so funny about that?"

"Nothing really, but the name's familiar and I can't remember where I've heard it before. I do remember that it had something to do with some bad time in my life. I have to say, though, I'm sort of glad I can't remember because I don't think those two guys had good intentions towards this Stephen Bryant fellow."

"How do you know?" Emily pulled out a pan of biscuits to finish preparing their supper.

"Well, I don't know for sure. But one of the guys, just in asking about this man, he had hatred burning in his eyes. Whoever this Stephen Bryant is, they've got it in for him."

Chapter 13

"The garden's growing fine!" Olivia announced as they came inside for lunch. "All the tomato rows are all perky and the beans and peas are up. The potatoes are showing their heads and the onions and garlic are, too."

"Will you get me a vase, Jane?" Lily asked, coming through the back door with her arms full of apple blossoms. The sweet fragrance filled the kitchen.

"Oh, my, did you get enough of those?" Mrs. Wellington looked on in surprise.

"Mm-hm." Lily filled the vase with water and arranged the boughs.

Mrs. Wellington smiled softly at her daughter's answer. They all knew Stephen would be joining them for supper that night.

"I'll be glad when this is done." Stephen straightened his back and wiped the sweat from his face. He and Will had been laboring for several days to get the foundation of Will's house dug.

"So will I—but for different reasons," Will chuckled as he steadily hacked away at the packed earth.

"You don't suppose we could manage two houses do you, Will?" Stephen thoughtfully continued his work.

"Not by ourselves. We'd have to hire help. Think you could afford materials, land and help?" Will asked, not surprised at his brother's question.

"I'm pretty close to affording it. I've got all the bounty added to what we've earned, so I think I could do it…"

"Got a piece of land picked out?"

"Yup." Stephen tossed another shovel full of dirt. "It's just northeast of Willow Pond. You know that spot where the land rises out of the valley and levels off for about half a mile or so before the Shadow Hills rise up? There are enough trees for shade and shelter from the wind…I'm gonna go see about it in Brockton on Saturday."

"Planning on talking to the marshal soon?"

"It's been on my mind…but I thought I'd wait a while longer…I'll be able to get everything in line, maybe even start building…and it'll give her some more time."

"You think she needs it?" Will asked.

Stephen didn't have time to answer. The brothers looked up at the sound of hoof beats.

"Hey, Darren…" Will waved as the mayor's son reined in his horse.

"Hi, guys, I heard you could use another strong back and pair of able hands."

"Yeah, thanks. I can't pay you much, though…"

"Whatever you can afford will be fine." Darren tethered his horse and untied the sack of tools he had brought.

"You came prepared," said Stephen, as Darren stepped into the trench next to him.

"Guess I didn't figure on being turned down."

Will was surprised when they finished digging the foundation that day. Darren's help had made an obvious difference.

"Feel like working permanently 'til late in the fall?" Stephen asked him as they packed up in the last light of sunset.

"Sure. You gonna start building, too?"

"Mm-hm—soon, I hope."

Dick and Beth's wedding took place on an unusually hot and sunny day for the second of June. Even though all the church windows were opened, the building was still very stuffy. Most of the ladies were fanning themselves.

While watching the giving of the bride and exchange of vows, Stephen was reminded of what he was hoping to do in the not too far future. He had been able to purchase the land for a house early in May and God had blessed his efforts so much that the house's foundation was already finished. With the help of several hired men, they were now working on the frame. He was glad to know that Will was making as much progress with his house. Shifting in his seat, he cast a side glance across the aisle at Lily, who sat intently watching the ceremony. He wondered what thoughts were occupying her mind. He had been fervently praying, asking God to lead him and Lily in the path He had for them. Nothing but peace and confidence filled his heart, as he knew they would bring more glory to God together than either of them could alone.

"I hope we can go swimming afterwards," Sarah whispered to Lily.

"I know..." Lily smiled as the new Mr. and Mrs. Richard Nelson were presented to their guests. It quickly turned into blushing when she caught Stephen's eye.

~~~

Summer was officially in season. Most days were hot and slightly humid. Lily welcomed the thunderstorms that sometimes roared through in the late afternoon or at night.

"The only problem is that you can't go out to splash in the puddles and get soaked," she mused, watching the lightning flicker one afternoon. "But the thunder *is* so wonderful."

More often, small rain showers quietly passed by, though they did not pour like the thunderstorms. The landscape seemed to be more revived and invigorated after their passing; the various shades of green intensified with the fresh rain.

A few weeks after Dick and Beth's wedding, Olivia was sitting under the shade of a maple tree fanning herself.

"I wonder if I'll ever get used to this overly hot weather. I'm positively dripping in sweat."

"I know, me too! Why don't we go swimming?" Jane asked.

"Lily's not here…"

"Well, she won't be back 'til Luke gets home, which'll be suppertime."

"Okay, let's go ask Mama." Olivia got up and her sister followed.

Mrs. Wellington readily gave her permission. "Just let me write a note for Lily in case she gets back before we do."

A few hours later, they returned just as Lily was reading the slip her mother had left.

"Couldn't you've stayed a little longer?" she sighed.

"Sorry, Dear, but we need to get to chores and I have to get supper figured out, too. How is Alice doing?"

"About the same. Her legs just get too weak and swollen from the weight of the baby. I did the laundry, dishes and helped keep Melly and Drew occupied, too. At least it's only a little more than a month before the baby comes—may I go down to the creek for a while to cool off?"

"Sure, the girls and I can get supper started."

Lily kicked off her shoes on the back steps and ran through the long grass to Willow Pond. The cool water was so refreshing that she waded in up to her knees. After she had cooled down a bit, Lily walked upstream to Whisper Springs. Deep purple violets graced the pool's edge and clustered around the rocks and trees that were in the small cove. Plucking some, Lily gathered a small bouquet. The woods' tranquil beauty and the water's quiet bubbling were soporific. Putting her elbows forward, she leaned on a large flat rock that was close to the pool's edge and let one hand lazily trail in the flowing water. The relaxing sound and feeling of the water plus the pleasant smell of violets began putting Lily to sleep.

Rustling grass and the sound of footsteps awakened her a little later. Expecting to see a woodland creature or one of her siblings, Lily looked up. To her surprise, she saw Stephen standing just a couple steps behind her.

"Hello…" Lily stirred from her relaxed position and stood up, wondering how he had found her.

"Your mama said you'd be here."

"I was helping Alice while the girls went swimming, so Mama said I could come up here for a while before supper…" Lily rambled and tried to keep her mind from wondering why he hadn't brought one of her siblings with him.

"Is Alice doing all right?"

"Mostly, yes, but she'll be relieved when the baby comes in August—I suppose Mama wants me back…" Lily started to take a step toward home, but Stephen stopped her.

"Lily…" he paused, trying to form on his lips words that were totally foreign.

Lily waited. The tone of his voice told her he had something important to say.

Stephen took both her hands in his. "I love you, Lily."

Shivers went down her spine and Lily felt her heart come in her throat as she looked into his dark eyes. There was no doubt in her mind whether or not she loved him. Yet she hadn't expected him to approach her, at least not yet.

Seeing her blue eyes look lovingly at him, the words easily formed on Stephen's lips. "Will you please marry me?"

Lily's lips parted in a smile as she gently squeezed the hands that held hers. "There's no one else I'd ever marry."

Stephen released her right hand and reached into the pocket of his pants. "I couldn't get you much, but I want to give you this as a promise of my love."

"Oh, Stephen, I don't need a promise..." Lily said quietly, letting him slide a gold ring of delicately worked filigree onto her finger.

"I don't want you to ever doubt how much I love you. I know the Lord has brought us together to bring glory to Him, and I'll always love only you."

Lily didn't respond, but her face radiated with trust.

Hand in hand, they followed the creek down the gentle slope and into the meadow.

"We're back," Lily called as she and Stephen came through the back door.

Mr. Wellington came from the sitting room with his arm around Mrs. Wellington. "Looks like our family's about to gain a son-in-law, Rachel," he told his wife, taking in Lily's glowing face.

Lily found herself wrapped first in her father's embrace, then in her mother's.

"It's a beautiful ring, Stephen," Mrs. Wellington admired.

"Where is everybody else?" Lily inquired, after noticing how alone the four of them were.

"Out in the barn. Why don't you go tell them?"

"All right."

"Remember those days?" Mrs. Wellington asked her husband, as they watched Lily and Stephen walk to the barn hand in hand.

"Yes. There is no doubt in my mind that they are made for each other."

"Like us?"

"Yes…like us." Mr. Wellington hugged her tightly.

"Oh, Lil…" Olivia almost immediately understood the glow on her sister's face.

"Are you getting married, too?" Mickey asked, trying to jump on Stephen's back.

"Yep…" Stephen flipped him over and swung him around.

"For real?" Johnny asked, putting his pitchfork in its place.

"Yes, for real..." Stephen laughed and swung Mickey onto his back for a ride, while all the young Wellington children danced and shouted for joy around them.

Danny returned home not long before the Bartons arrived to join the family for supper. When Stephen and Lily told him their news, Danny wrapped Stephen in a brotherly hug.

"My lil' sister..." were his soft words to Lily, as she received his warm embrace.

Later, when she was finally in bed that night, Lily mulled over the day's events in her mind, reliving every moment and every word Stephen had spoken to her by the creek, treasuring every part of it.

~~~

"Do you think you're up to taking a trip, Emily?" Ben asked one night at supper.

"I think I can manage it. Where do you want to go?" Emily looked away from Amelia's food in surprise.

"Oakville. It's northwest of here. I'd like to stop by the prison on the way, too, if you're all right with that."

Emily nodded somewhat hesitantly.

"If you don't want to go, we don't have to. I just thought it might be nice to get away, and I feel like I owe Jack a visit, as well as Marshal Wellington."

"I think it would be fine to go. It's just the prison part."

"We wouldn't go into the prison cells. They'd bring whoever we want to see out. I'd like you to meet Jack Thomas."

"All right."

A week and a half later, they got into their buggy and drove the thirteen miles to the State Prison.

"Ben!" Jack's eyes almost popped out when he saw his old comrade.

"Hi, Jack!" Ben firmly grasped his friend's hand.

"You ol' rascal!" Jack exclaimed, slapping Ben on the shoulder when he introduced Emily and Amelia. "You'd marry a pretty one, too, wouldn't ya?"

Emily blushed slightly at the compliment.

"You wouldn't be against my holding that sweet little baby, would you, Ma'am?" Jack sheepishly asked her.

"No, I wouldn't mind in the least and call me Emily." Emily passed her little girl into his oversized arms.

"Can't say I've ever held something so sweet and beautiful." With a well-worked hand that was amazingly careful for its large size, Jack gently touched Amelia's soft cheek.

"How's the work goin', Jack?" Ben brought up the subject that was heavy on his mind.

"Well, I'm not complaining 'cause God's in control…Mitch was saved not long after you left, but Rex, oh, he's a hard one. He's convinced that no one could love him, let alone die for him. Two other prisoners asked the Lord to save 'em. Both of 'em were old and on their death beds. Several of the guards—some of the worst ones, in fact. Mostly all the rest insist that 'religion' is for sissy's an' don't want nothin' to do with it. They're a hard bunch—tough as nails and dumb as oxen. Some o' them get violent over my Sunday preachin' and op'n singin'—Ray Trent's still a huge problem." He added in an undertone. "They might let me out on probation just 'cause of the way him and some of those fellers act."

"If they do, you head straight for our place in Lyndale. Our home is your home," Ben ordered.

"You bet."

They stayed for almost three more hours. Jack brought Ben around to meet the new converts. Several of the unsaved prisoners recognized Ben and muttered curses as he passed by. They left long after lunch time and made it to the Charleston Station in time to board the night train.

~~~

A silver star gleamed in the morning sun as the marshal strode along the boardwalk, intently watching everything around him. The hired wagon from the Brockton train station was not an unusual sight, but the man driving it caught Mr. Wellington by surprise. With a long sprint, he crossed the street to Mrs. Ellis' Boarding House where the wagon had stopped.

"Ben Hanson," he said, after the man helped the lady in the wagon down. In a moment, the former outlaw was facing him.

"Marshal." Ben gave Mr. Wellington's hand a hearty shake.

"What're you doing here?"

"Came to see you. Figured it was high time. Two years is a long while. Thought I'd give you proof that God's work is not in vain—this is my wife, Emily, our daughter, Amelia, and we're also expecting another child."

"I'm very pleased to meet you. God's wonders never cease, do they, Ben?" the marshal looked at Emily, who held their baby girl.

"Nope. Praise His name, God's done so much since I left two years ago."

"He hasn't stopped working here either—tell you what, you get settled in at Mary's and then you can take Emily out to our place—you know how to get there—then if you want, you can come back here and we'll catch up."

"Sounds good to me," Ben nodded.

"Somebody's here, Mama!" Jane came through the back door.

"Who?" Mrs. Wellington asked, going to the front.

"I don't know. Strangers."

"Hello," Mrs. Wellington gave a friendly smile as the unfamiliar couple got out of a rig. "May I help you?"

"I don't know if you remember me, Ma'am, I'm Ben Hanson. This is my wife, Emily, and our daughter, Amelia."

"Oh, my!" Mrs. Wellington gasped. "I never imagined we'd meet again—I'm so pleased to meet you, Emily. Won't you both come inside? Does Michael know you're here?"

"We saw him first thing. I'll be going back to see him now. He invited me to drop off Emily," said Ben, as they walked up to the door.

"Well, I'm very glad he did."

When Ben had taken his leave, Emily shyly apologized, "I'm sorry, I feel like I'm imposing."

"Not in the least. You're most welcome. In fact, I'm so excited to see the answer to our prayers and I want to hear all about it." Mrs. Wellington motioned for her to sit down. "You can come here children," she said, seeing several pairs of eyes peeping around a corner. Emily's eyes widened as she was introduced to the ten children that came from the kitchen and upstairs.

"You have ten children," she stated amazed.

"Twelve actually. Our oldest, Luke is married and then Danny is working as a doctor."

"I've always dreamed of having a large family."

"Well, God's the one who gives us such blessings. I can see He's been blessing you." Mrs. Wellington smiled and nodded to Emily's slightly protruding figure. "Would you like something to drink?"

"No, thank you, I'm fine."

Their conversation easily opened into what had transpired years before and how Emily and Ben had come to be where they were at the present.

"That almost sounds like a fairy tale," Sarah said, when Emily had finished telling how she and Ben had gotten married.

"Almost," Emily laughed softly.

~~~

"Hey, Danny, I've got somebody to see you." Mr. Wellington walked into the doctor's clinic with Ben Hanson.

"Can you have Doc Barton see him, Pa? I was just about to go out on my—" Danny stopped short when he came through the drapes with his saddlebag slung over his shoulder and saw who was with his father.

"Ben Hanson! Where in the world did you come from?"

"Southeast hills—hey, Danny," Ben did not hesitate to take Danny's outstretched hand.

"What's all this?" Dr. Barton came out of the backroom.

"Tom, you remember Ben Hanson from the night our house was on fire," said the marshal.

"Maybe…he was the one who got Rachel and the kids out, right?"

"Right." Ben nodded.

"He's also the one, as I recall, who you got Arnon to pardon against everyone's better judgment, which—it turns out, I see—was the wise choice. Glad to see you, Ben."

"You're comin' to supper aren't you?" Danny asked.

"Your pa's already seen to that."

"He's married now, Danny...has a baby girl, Amelia, and one on the way, too. They're at our house now," Mr. Wellington told him.

"Well, I'll be...wish I could stick around, but...I've got to check on Alice and Isabella. Issy's still a little colicky and I should check on how Alice is doing. But I'll see you tonight, bye." Danny walked out with a quick step.

Dinner took a long time that night. There was so much to talk about.

"I see you took the opportunity and expanded the kitchen after the fire," Ben commented.

"It's been nice. I'm glad the Bryants suggested it." Mr. Wellington was surprised how openly Ben talked about that horrifying night.

"Bryants?" Ben repeated, surprise in his voice as he glanced at his wife.

"William and Stephen. Tom Barton is their father now. Their mother remarried after she was widowed, but the boys have kept their father's last name."

"Ben?" Emily looked at her husband with a little bit of worry.

"I thought I'd find him if I came back here, Em."

Everyone around the table looked at the Hansons in confusion.

"A while ago, a couple men stopped by the blacksmith's shop where I work in Lyndale. They were asking if anyone had heard of a Stephen Bryant," Ben explained. "I didn't remember where I'd heard the name before, so I couldn't help them. That's partially why we came up. I wanted to place that name. Something about it all bothered me."

"Why?" Mr. Wellington questioned.

"Because I don't think they had good intentions, that's why."

"What'd they look like?"

"One was tall and skinny, the other was shorter and heavier. The shorter one wore a faded Confederate cap."

"Hmm...probably some old grudge...I'll take you over there after supper. Wanna come too, Lil?"

"You bet I do."

Dr. Barton leisurely rose from his chair and answered the knock on their front door. "Hi, Mike...Ben...Lily, what brings you around so late?"

"Hi, Tom, is Stephen in? We came by to talk to him."

"Sure, I'll call him. Why don't you sit down..." Dr. Barton's face showed his curiosity as he motioned them to the kitchen table. Mrs. Barton and the girls were occupying the sitting room with their various evening projects.

The tramping of Stephen's boots down the stairs answered the doctor's call.

He saw his visitors as he entered the kitchen and recognized Ben almost immediately. "Hi, Lily...Mr. Wellington...and Mr. Hanson." He shook Ben's hand.

"We came over to talk with you a few minutes, Stephen. It seems that a couple guys are looking for you," Mr. Wellington went straight to the point.

"Looking for me?" Stephen raised his eyebrows.

"Mm-hm." Ben retold what had happened.

By the time he was done, Stephen was very sober.

"You didn't tell them?"

"No, I honestly didn't know where it was I knew you from," Ben asserted.

"Who are they?" Mr. Wellington asked.

"Brett Whitney and Arnold Setters," Stephen groaned out the words.

"What do they want, Stephen?" Lily tried to keep the fear she felt out of her voice.

"In sixty-four, at Cold Harbor, Brett—a corporal at the time—started taking his unit of men around to flank the left side of Grant's army, which, besides being suicidal to all of his men, was against orders. I knew it was against orders because my group was given the same ones as Brett. I couldn't believe it when I saw it. I don't think he understood what he was going into. Being his senior officer, I basically took control of his unit as well as mine and forced him to comply. It only added to the grudge he had against me. See, even though I was younger than him and I had enlisted later, I received a promotion before he did.

"When our troops surrendered to Grant, I unintentionally aggravated him more. He threatened afterwards that he'd find me some day and get even—but I never gave it a second thought…Arnold's always been close to Brett…and there were a few times I had to pull rank on him. So I guess he sees it as his fight, too…I'd never thought that after all this time…" he sighed out his last sentence.

"Well…we'll just have to pray the Lord thwarts all their efforts," Mr. Wellington stated.

"Yeah…that's for sure…" Stephen felt Lily's hand tighten around his.

Chapter 14

"What do you think about this one, Mama?" Lily held up a bolt of soft white muslin. They were shopping in Brockton for the last necessities for the wedding.

"That's perfect...where'd you find it?"

"Way up on the top shelf."

"No wonder we didn't see it," said Olivia.

They brought the bolt down for the clerk to cut the desired length. Meanwhile, they picked out lace trimming and ribbons for Lily's veil and bonnet.

"Well...the Lord certainly blessed us today. We've gotten the last of the things we need and all in a fairly quick amount of time. I didn't expect such success," Mrs. Wellington commented, as they stepped outside later and got into the wagon.

"Hope Stephen's making as much progress on the house as we are on the wedding things," Lily pondered aloud with a light heart.

Her hopes were dashed, though, that evening when Stephen joined them for supper. "I've got bad news, Lil," he began, when they sat in the living room after dessert.

"What is it?"

"I'm afraid we'll have to postpone the wedding."

"Why?"

"I've run out of savings and we've only just finished the framework and floors…I wasn't planning on the Charlettedale Mill raising their prices. I thought of taking my business elsewhere, but it wouldn't be worth it to go an extra thirty-seven miles south to the Ashton Mill…"

"Couldn't we just work something out like Will and Anna did? With the boarding house?"

"I'd rather not…the only money I have is what's coming in from our carpentry work. I don't expect to start out rich, but I'd like to have something to fall back on if we need to."

Lily struggled with mixed feelings, knowing he was right and yet not wanting to wait. Though they had said nothing, she knew her parents were in agreement. Stephen was taking his responsibility of providing for her very seriously.

"How much more would we need?" she finally asked.

"To finish it like I want to I've estimated almost fifty dollars," Stephen answered.

"Oh, my!" Mrs. Wellington spoke for the first time.

"How long do you think it will take, Stephen?" Mr. Wellington queried.

"At least until the spring. More likely 'til next fall—I'm sorry, Lily...but I don't see any other way we could do it."

"It's okay...you're right." Lily tried to be brave and hide her extreme disappointment. "It's the right thing to do. We'll wait. God will provide."

In spite of her valiant words, Lily's heart was heavy. Silently, she cried in bed that night, begging God to provide a way for them to marry sooner.

But if it is not Your will, Lord, help me to be patient and strong. Help me to trust with full faith that You know what's best. Then with peace in her soul, Lily fell asleep.

It was a few days later. Lily was reorganizing her dresser. She was working on the small top drawer where she kept her special things. One by one, she lifted out each item and placed it on top of the dresser. Reaching deep into the back of the drawer, she pulled out the velvet box that her locket had come in. From underneath the box, her eye caught a glimpse of something grayish-colored on the drawer's bottom.

Curiously, she reached back and to her surprise felt several pieces of paper. Pulling a few out, she gasped in wonder. Five dollar bills! Excitedly, she pulled out several more.

"Oh, thank You, Lord!" Lily cried, racing from the room. "Mama! Mama! Look what I found!"

"What?" Mrs. Wellington looked up from the plants she was watering.

"Fifty dollars! I forgot all about it! It's the reward money Stephen insisted that I take back when the Bailey brothers robbed the bank!"

Lily ran all the way to Will's house, where she knew Stephen would be.

"Will…where's Stephen?" she asked breathlessly, surprised he wasn't there.

"He's over at his house, well, your house too, I guess. Said he was just going to finish a few things and close it up sort of 'til we can work on it again. What's the big news?" It was obvious on Lily's face that something wonderful had happened.

"We don't have to wait! I have the money we need!" Lily started running again. Her sides were aching when she came in sight of the half-finished house. "Stephen!" she barely managed to yell, she was so out of breath. At her voice, Stephen looked up.

"What is it, Lil?" he asked as she ran up to him.

"God's answered our prayers!" She paused a moment for breath. "He provided the way a whole year ago when you shot the Baileys!" Almost bursting with joy, Lily's eyes filled with tears as she extended the folded green bills.

"What?" Stephen was incredulous as he took them from her hand.

"It's the fifty dollars reward money that you sneaked into my purse!" Lily explained.

Stephen flipped through the cash twice before responding with a loud "Yaahoo! We can do it, Lil! God answered and gave us the way even before we asked." He swung her off the ground in a joyous embrace.

"He's promised He will provide exceedingly abundantly!" Lily glowed.

"You never tried to give the money back..." Stephen said after a thoughtful pause.

"I wanted to so bad. You'll never know how angry I was when I found it in my purse. But Mama said I shouldn't because it might offend you. So I saved it. I don't know exactly why I didn't use any of it...guess I felt like it would be a waste to spend it on something I didn't really need when somebody else might need it more someday." She thoughtfully paused before continuing. "I think God purposely put us through this...and tested us to see if we would make the hard, but wise decision of waiting another year to get married. I think He wanted to test and strengthen our obedience...and our faith in Him."

"Yeah, and I also think," Stephen said, extending his hand which Lily readily took, "that He put us through this to teach us how to trust each other and learn to work together better. He gave me the experience of being a strong leader...no matter how hard the decision was for me to wait and not take out a loan."

"He also tested me in being submissive and supportive to your leadership," Lily put in.

With fondness, Stephen smiled. "My parents say that after years of living together you only learn to love each other more. But the way I love you now, I wonder how that's possible…"

~~~

Lily couldn't remember a busier summer. Amidst the gardening and canning, they somehow managed to pull together her dress and all the wedding plans. Often she felt as if there was always so much to do, and yet at the same time she wished it would never end. Lily found herself longing for each day to stretch on forever at the realization that she would soon be leaving her family to make a home of her own with Stephen.

"Was it hard for you to leave home when you married Papa?" Lily asked, as she and her mother sat together working on her dress.

"Not terribly. I knew I would miss my parents, but I was ready for life's change. Your uncle Bert had already gone wayward, so it was just me at home…it's strange how marriage is so bittersweet. I think it'll be a lot harder for you because you have all your brothers and sisters that you're so close to."

"You wouldn't mind if I came over every day, would you?" Lily stopped her tedious stitching to look at her mother.

"You know you don't have to ask that, my Lily of the Valley." Mrs. Wellington gently touched her daughter's face. "At the same time…I don't doubt how much you love Stephen, but you need to be sure to keep your relationship with him above all other earthly relationships. Now that doesn't mean you shut us out or love us any less—it just means that your priorities change. We come second—and Stephen's first. You are leaving us to cleave to him. Don't come to me or Papa or anyone else for advice if you haven't already talked and prayed with Stephen about it. One of the most dangerous things for a marriage is not communicating. Honestly tell him what you think and how you feel about things…if there's an offense, don't get angry and silent—talk to him…if it's something you feel God is calling you both to do, tell him…if he's doing something that you don't think is right—tell him. But always do it in love and with a meek and gentle spirit."

Praying to God for wisdom and strength, Lily hid all her mother's counsel deep in her heart.

~~~

The Wellington family didn't know where the summer went. Before they knew it, the week of October seventh had come around. Their already active house seemed to turn into a whirlwind. In the middle of the week, Stephen announced that they had finished the house. Lily begged to go see it, for she hadn't seen it ever since the day she'd brought Stephen the reward money.

Stephen shook his head, saying: "You can see it on Saturday, my bride."

Lily quietly complied without another word, though she ached to see their new home. She wanted to give him the pleasure of showing it to her as he desired.

The eve of the wedding came all too quickly. As she climbed in bed, Lily fought to keep her mind still so she could sleep. It was well past midnight when, after much prayer, she was able to calm her excitement and let the morrow take care of itself.

Though she'd been up late into the night, Lily was awake at sunrise the next morning. Quietly, she prayed for a blessing on the day and watched the eastern sunrays wash the room in pink light. Not long after, everyone else in the house was up and preparing for the day ahead of them.

Even though she was the bride, Lily still aided the cleanup of breakfast and helped her younger siblings with their clothes.

"You should really come get ready yourself, Lil," Olivia told her.

"I will," Lily responded, wiping one last counter.

Shivers went up and down her spine as she pulled on her creamy dress shoes and slid the snowy organza gown over her head.

"We have decided that we are going to style your hair," Jane emphatically announced, to Lily's surprise.

"Okay, if you insist. Then I can do yours."

Sitting her down in front of the mirror, Olivia and Jane went to work twisting, tucking and pinning. She was very pleased with the end result. The thick mass of Lily's hair was pinned on the crown of her head in princess-like style. They had pulled out tendrils of Lily's hair at the sides of her neck and curled them.

"Now for the finishing touch…" Jane lifted the veil from its box. Small shimmering beads were wrapped around the headpiece and the soft tulle floated through the air as she brought it to Lily's head. Olivia secured it.

"All right, Jane, it's time to do your hair," Lily said, rising from her seat in front of the mirror.

She was just finishing Olivia's hair, when Mrs. Wellington came in fully dressed and ready.

"Livy and Jane, are you ready to go with Danny and I?" she asked.

Olivia stood and she and Jane left with their things as Mrs. Wellington stepped toward Lily. Unshed tears filled her eyes as she looked on her daughter's radiant appearance.

"I told myself I wouldn't cry for your sake, but I guess it's no use," she sniffed slightly as she embraced Lily. "I knew this day would come, and I wanted it to…but I wish it hadn't come so fast."

"I know…" Lily blinked away her own tears.

"We're ready, Mama," Danny called up the stairs.

"I'm coming," Mrs. Wellington hugged Lily closely once more. "I'll see you in a little while."

With a shaky sigh, Lily sat on her bed after Mrs. Wellington had departed from the room. *I never thought I could feel this way: terribly excited and happy, but at the same time deeply sad and almost dreading leaving my family...I love Stephen with all my heart, and want to be his wife, but this is so hard to leave my family, even though we're only going to be living a couple miles away...Heavenly Father, would You please ease the pain? Let me only feel the joy of all You've done for Stephen and me? Knit our hearts together, Lord, may we honor You in our life together as we become one today.*

Lily looked up at her father's footsteps, as he came into the room.

"Here we are..." the marshal fought to keep his own feelings in check. "Your wedding day...where did the time go? Just yesterday you were my little girl, begging for me to hold you. Now look at you...a beautiful bride. There is no man on earth I would rather give you to than Stephen Bryant." His voice was unsteady. "Remember that no matter how sad and brokenhearted I may seem to be today, I'm not regretting this in the least. Even the tears and sadness of your leaving cannot compare to the joy I have in seeing you married to Stephen."

Lily hugged him tightly. "I love you so much, Papa."

Together they prayed for a blessing on the day and marriage, that God's glory would be seen.

It was just the Bartons there when Danny, Mrs. Wellington and the others arrived at the church. Jane immediately sat at the piano to lay out her music. She had been thrilled when Lily asked her to play the music, saying Jane was more than capable.

As she gave Rachel one last rehearsal in walking down the aisle in front of her and showed her how thickly she should lay the wildflower petals, Olivia wondered if she was ready herself. She prayed she wouldn't cry until the day was over.

Guests soon began arriving. Praying her clammy fingers would work and that tears wouldn't blur her music, Jane began the prelude.

As Rachel and Olivia slipped out the doors to prepare for the processional with Sarah, Lily and Mr. Wellington pulled into the churchyard.

"Here we go," the marshal said, lifting her out of the buggy. "Pray my resolve holds."

"Mine, too." Lily smiled and it seemed to drive away the pain of the coming separation. "Ready, Liv?" she looked at her younger sister.

"Ready as I'll ever be." There was only the faintest trace of tears in Olivia's eyes.

Mr. Wellington pulled the veil over Lily's face and took her arm as they waited for Jane's cue. The moment it came, Lily felt her heartbeat quicken.

"Here we go," she whispered, as Olivia opened the doors and Rachel began walking into the church just as she had practiced.

Lily reminded herself this was not all a dream, as she watched her sisters slowly proceed before her as she walked down the aisle holding her father's arm. Everyone standing and watching her seemed to blur into nothing when Stephen's face came into view. Her breath caught in her throat then and with great effort, she forced herself to relax.

Stopping with her father in front of the pulpit, she waited as Jane ended the song and Mr. Grey began the ceremony by asking by whose authority she was given to this man. A moment after the marshal answered for himself and his wife, the veil's white haze was lifted and he gently kissed Lily's forehead before slipping her hand into Stephen's and stepping to the side. Together they faced Mr. Grey and he continued with the ceremony.

With the congregation as their witness, Lily and Stephen gave their solemn vows to each other.

"With the authority that's vested in me, I now pronounce you man and wife—Stephen, you may kiss your bride." In a moment, Lily felt Stephen's arms around her and his lips gently pressed a kiss on hers. As she pulled back, Lily's shining eyes met Stephen's. Then she knew it was real. They were one at last.

Turning to face their audience, Mr. Grey spoke, "Ladies and Gentlemen, I present to you Mr. and Mrs. Stephen Bryant."

Their joyful audience clapped as they walked down the aisle and then everyone followed them outside to the churchyard.

Out of deference, their families were given time to say goodbye before everybody sent them off. The Wellingtons waited for the Bartons to have their goodbyes first. Lily didn't have to fight to keep from crying until she faced her siblings. No matter how hard she tried, persistent tears trickled down her cheeks as she embraced each of her brothers and sisters.

"Oh, my Lily..." Rachel Wellington held her daughter tightly. "I love you so...and I'm so thankful to God for the woman you've become."

"I have a wonderful example in you, Mama."

Her mother gave a small laugh. "Thank you...you'd best hug your papa. You've got plenty of guests waiting to congratulate you. I love you."

"I love you, too." Lily smiled before she turned to her father.

Michael Wellington brushed a tear from her cheek before tightly enfolding her in his arms. "I love you..." her father kissed the side of her face before releasing her, so she could bid farewell to the guests.

"I love you. Where's Danny?" Lily asked, quickly wiping away her tears.

"Bringing the buggy around."

As Stephen and Lily bade the rest of the people farewell, Danny stood waiting with the buggy. Through a shower of wheat berries, Stephen and Lily ran to meet him.

"Bye, Lil..." Danny's voice shook slightly as he hugged his sister.

"Bye, Danny," Lily's arms tightened around his neck. "I love you so much."

"I love you, too...you'd better leave before you're buried in wheat." Danny smiled, recovering his sense of humor. Lily laughed, too, in spite of herself. Stephen helped her into the buggy, then turned to say his own goodbye to Danny.

"See you in a few days, Danny," Stephen said as they gave each other a big embrace.

"Yeah...I couldn't have asked for a better brother-in-law. There's no one better for Lil." Danny held the reins as Stephen climbed up next to his bride. Then handing them to Stephen, Danny slapped the horses' hind quarters.

Final farewells were called out as the horses lurched forward. Lily and Stephen turned back and waved until they were shrouded from view by the trees lining the road. Wiping the tears from her eyes, Lily turned around and sighed.

"Ready to go home?" Stephen asked with a smile.

Lily didn't catch the meaning in his question right away. "Oh! Home! My new home. Yes! I finally get to see it—everything's whirling around me so, I forgot about it. I must be a sight—bawling like this."

"You are a sight. A very pretty one." Stephen smiled, sliding his arm around her. "Now when I say so, you'll have to close your eyes and not open them 'til I say you can."

"If you say so. Were you able to finish it just like the diagrams you showed me?" Even though Lily hadn't understood the drawings completely, she had a faint idea of what the house should look like.

"You'll see."

"You won't even give me a small hint?" Lily pleaded, turning her head to look at him.

"Nope, you'll just have to be patient and see when we get there."

"Well, since I haven't seen it in weeks, I guess a few more minutes won't hurt."

"Actually, it's almost an hour's ride."

"Well, anyway, I can wait."

Stephen laughed. "I love you, Lily." They drove on for a ways before he spoke again. "What should I call you?"

"What do you mean?"

"A pet name, like 'darling' or 'sweetheart'—I don't want to call you Lily all the time. It's too normal and not...endearing enough."

"Love."

"What?"

It was Lily's turn to laugh. "'Love'—sometimes Papa calls Mama that. I've always liked the sound of it. 'Love' or 'my love'...or you could do 'my Lil' or—I don't know. Anything you come up with that suits your fancy, I guess. It'll make it more special for me that way. Or shouldn't I give you that liberty because you might come up with something silly?"

"Don't you trust me?"

"Almost to a fault, I think..."

"It's funny that you should mention 'Love' for a pet name...my first pa called Mama that."

"Really?" Lily laid her head on his shoulder at the look of pain that crossed Stephen's face.

It didn't feel like an hour before Stephen told Lily she had to shut her eyes.

"...and if you peek," he paused to think. "Well, just don't peek and then I won't have to think of some punishment."

Lily laughed and shut her eyes. Several minutes later, she felt the buggy slow down and turn slightly to the left. Then they stopped.

"Can I open my eyes now?" she asked.

"No, not 'til I say so."

All Lily's senses were tingling with anticipation. She felt the buggy wiggle as Stephen got down. Then his hands were lifting her up and setting her on the ground.

"Now?" Lily couldn't wait to hear his permission.

"No, hang on." Stephen took her hand and led her several steps.

Lily felt his hand let go of hers and heard him take a step away. "Where're you going?"

"I'm still here...okay, you can open them now."

The look of wonder that came into her eyes filled Stephen with deep pleasure.

Three shuttered windows framed the upper level of the house. The ground level's exterior was unique in that the door was not centered. Instead, it was on the right side of the porch. On the far left side was a swing, and a picture window was between it and the door.

"Stephen, it's so beautiful! Where'd you ever find the time and wood to even make a swing?" his bride asked in awe, when she was able to take her eyes away from the home he had built for her.

"We had some scraps when everything else was done. It was Susie's idea. And I know you love swings. Ready to see inside?"

"Of course!" Before Lily could move forward, she was swept off her feet in Stephen's arms and carried to the house. The new oak boards thudded soundly as he mounted the porch steps.

"Go ahead, open it," he said, stopping in front of the door. Without hesitation, Lily reached out and turned the cast iron knob.

"Welcome home, Lil," Stephen said softly, as the door swung open to reveal a spacious sitting room. To the left of the kitchen door was a wide brick hearth, on the other side of which Lily spotted a second entry to the kitchen. On the far left side of the room was a flight of steps leading upstairs.

After crossing the threshold, Stephen set Lily on her feet. She gazed around the room. The sofa and armchairs their parents had bought as a wedding present were already in place.

"Come, let me show you." Stephen took her hand and led her into the room.

After showing Lily the kitchen and sitting room, both stacked with crates of dishes and other home necessities, Stephen led her to the four bedrooms of which the upstairs consisted. One of the front facing bedrooms was already furnished. The bed was perfectly centered between the two windows and a bureau was situated on the opposite wall.

"Stick your head out and see the view." Stephen opened one of the windows and Lily leaned out. The hills were in back of the house and from the window she could see the small cove in its valley with the meadow in the far distance.

"Like it?" Stephen asked a moment before Lily pulled her head in.

"I've never seen anything so wonderful." Lily's voice was just above a whisper as she looked back at him. "Thank you so much! It's perfect."

Stephen took her hands in his and together they bowed their heads. Thanking God for the day, he prayed that the Lord would forever be with them, drawing them closer together for God's glory.

Chapter 15

Blowing stray hairs out of her face, Lily straightened and brushed fragments of hay from her skirt. She had just finished unpacking, organizing and putting away the last of the dishes and food supplies. Everything was finally where she wanted it to be, but what a task it had been!

Footsteps brought her around to face the door.

"Need any help?" Stephen inquired.

"Sure, you can take care of these empty crates…and then if you want, you can help me put the last few things in the sitting room."

"Okay, but I doubt I'll be much help decorating. I don't have a very creative eye." He grabbed the four crates, two in each hand, and left to deposit them outside. On his return, he found Lily upstairs in the other bedroom that faced the front yard.

"I thought the big chest could stay in here under the window for now," Lily began telling him her ideas. "I'd like the big braided rug from Mrs. Ellis in the sitting room." She pointed to the dense floor spread. "Then I wanted Grampa Charles' rocking chair up here...well, no, it should stay downstairs—never mind. Hmm..." she thought for a moment. "The candlesticks from Uncle Mark and Aunt Pearl and the doilies from Mrs. Evans will be perfect to put on the mantel. For now, will you carry the rug down, please?" Lily picked up the few lighter items she wanted and followed Stephen out of the room.

"Are you and Will really busy?" Lily asked as they laid out the rug.

"Not really busy, but we're busy enough. Why?"

"Well...I'm probably getting too ahead of myself—but those rooms upstairs feel so empty. Would it be too much to make a bed for at least two of them?"

"I'll see how it goes. Will and I still have to raise ourselves barns by the first snow."

"Oh, yeah...well, it's not a necessity, so it can wait." Lily placed the silver candlesticks on doilies at either end of the mantle. "What do you think?"

"Looks like home," Stephen said with a smile.

~~~

Lily looked in the window of the Charlettedale milliner shop late one afternoon. On one of the display stands rested the most beautiful bonnet she had ever seen in her entire life.

"Well, hello, Lily," a creamy voice turned Lily from the window.

"Oh, hi, Lauren. How are you doing?" Lauren Collins was the last person Lily had expected to see.

"I'm fine, thank you. I was just about to go in, so I'll join you. That is if you were going in and not just window shopping. I hope your circumstances haven't reduced you to that."

"No, not at all. I just asked Stephen if I could come along while he went to the mill." Lily bristled at the young woman's degrading pity. "But I have no need of a new bonnet."

"Every lady needs a beautiful hat and more than just one, I say. One bonnet can't possibly coordinate with every dress you own!" Lauren took Lily's arm and led her through the shop's door. She seemed intent on having Lily's company, and Lily was enthralled with the silk bonnet.

There were other women in the store as the bell jingled their entrance. Lily felt herself immediately immersed in the feminine styles.

"May I help you with something?" a clerk asked her.

"No, thank you, I'm just looking," Lily said kindly.

Lauren interjected, "Looking indeed. I saw you eyeing that white silk with the blue flowers. But I realize that it costs more than your husband probably allows you. Such a pity, too, as the blue of the flowers is a perfect match to your eyes."

Lauren Collins, you're just trying to humiliate me and Stephen, aren't you…well, I'll prove we aren't so poor, Lily thought as she spoke, "How much is the white silk with the blue flowers in the window display?"

"Six dollars and eighty-nine cents. But I'm afraid we only have that one and it's been claimed. However, we have ordered two more, which I expect to come in on Thursday. If you pay half price now, we'll reserve one for you and you can pay the rest when you come to get it day after tomorrow."

Something pulled at Lily's heart as she agreed and gave the clerk the money. But she forgot it the moment she saw Lauren's surprised face. The price was well worth it to put Lauren Collins in her rightful place. Lily was still enjoying the satisfaction of it when she met Stephen at the Charlettedale Mill.

"So what'd you do?" Stephen asked as they drove out of town.

"I went window shopping—well, not completely," she hesitated. "I did get one thing."

"What is it?"

"A bonnet."

"A bonnet?" There was an edge to his voice that Lily didn't like.

"I didn't get it yet," Lily went on, hoping it meant nothing. "I had to reserve it. You should've seen the shocked look on Lauren Collins' face. She thought she'd pinned me into a corner where she could push me into an embarrassing position and degrade me with false pity."

"How much was it?" The edge was still there.

"Six eighty-nine, but I only had to pay three forty-five to reserve one they have coming in."

"We can't afford to spend that much, Lil."

Even though his tone was gentle, Lily felt a sharp rebuke. "Well, I *was* just window shopping until Lauren came along and pressured me into going into the store and buying it." She tried to justify herself.

"*You're* responsible for your actions and our savings, Lil, not Lauren."

"Well, I wasn't going to have her shaming you by saying you can't provide for us and afford a bonnet," Lily responded heatedly.

"If she thinks that—it's her problem. She's got a lot to learn if she thinks that more than one bonnet's an absolute necessity."

"But you know how the Collins' girls gossip. Don't you care about what others might think?"

"To a certain extent—yes." Stephen was a little surprised at Lily's seemingly vehement concern about what people thought of them. "But I'm not going to spend money we need, just to keep people from talking. And in a way, Lauren is right…we can't afford a bonnet. The income is needed more on food and other necessities."

"So you're saying I was foolish?"

"You shouldn't have let Lauren bother you. It doesn't matter what she thinks." Stephen sensed tension between them. "It's all right, Lil. We'll manage somehow."

Lily didn't reply. The rest of the ride home was silent.

During the next two days, the bonnet incident seemed to be forgotten. But Thursday night quickly brought it into conversation.

"What's this, Lil?" Stephen sat at the table going over their account.

"What's what?" Lily leaned over his shoulder.

"This second payment for the bonnet from the milliner in Charlettedale?" Stephen pointed to the neat record Lily had made.

"Well, I told you. It cost six eighty-nine, but I had to pay half on Tuesday to reserve it and then the rest today when I picked it up."

"Oh...I thought you said that it only cost half the original price..." Stephen's voice was almost a groan. "It was one thing for the price to be almost four dollars, but almost seven...Lil...seven dollars for a bonnet? How could you do that?" Frustration colored his voice.

"Well, I told you what happened."

"I know, but that's no excuse. I can't believe you let Lauren get to you so much as to spend such an amount on a bonnet. A bonnet! I thought you knew how to handle money." Stephen's voice rose.

"I do! If you had her in your ear prodding you into the store and then telling the clerk that you were eyeing the display...just setting you up for humiliation and embarrassment, you'd buy it just to spite her, too," Lily defensively replied.

"That doesn't justify it, Lil. It was foolish and prideful, the way a child responds. It was wrong of you. Why couldn't you have let it go? This price was not worth it."

"Well, maybe I am just a foolish girl who has a lot of growing up to do still!" Lily stalked out of the room and Stephen heard her footsteps retreating up the stairs. With a heavy sigh, he leaned his elbows on the table. *I shouldn't have jumped on her like that...wasn't the right way to handle it at all. Lord, please forgive me and help me to make it right.*

Lily kicked the door of the empty front bedroom shut. In anger, she sat on the large chest and hugged her knees as she looked out at the October night sky. *How dare he talk to me like that?* she fumed.

It was a while before her resistance broke down. It hurt to have him angry with her. It hurt even more to know he was right. She knew she had let her foolish pride control her actions—that the whole thing was her fault.

Oh, Lord, I'm sorry. Cleanse me of my pride. I don't want pride to separate me and You, and I definitely don't want to be shut away from Stephen. Show me a way to make it right, Lily prayed, blinking away a tear. When she heard the soft scuff of Stephen's boots at the door, she wondered how she'd ever apologize to him and tell him how sorry she was.

The door knob clicked. Stephen crossed the room and knelt by the chest. In shame, Lily didn't turn from the window. She still couldn't face him.

"I'm sorry I was so short with you, Lil…" Stephen hesitated, laying a hand on hers.

Finally, Lily turned her head to face him. "I was so awful to you. Totally thoughtless. You were right. It was all just my foolish pride. I was acting like a spoiled little girl. Can you forgive me?"

Stephen pulled her into his arms. "Of course, I forgive you. We'll make do somehow."

The next day, Lily was pulling a pie and tarts out of the oven when Stephen came into the house.

"It never fails," he said, tossing his tattered hat on the table. "When it rains, it pours."

"What happened?" Lily looked curiously at the tears and holes in his hat, and smears on his shirt.

"I went to Joe Patterson's to pick up the scrap lumber he had. You know how their dogs are rather unruly? Well, they have a new one—Rex—I don't think he's a dog at all. He's a bear or part wolf or something..."

Lily laughed at his description.

"Anyway, Rex hasn't learned how to treat visitors yet. The minute I got down from the wagon, he was on me—knocked off my hat and everything. He made the other dogs think it was playtime and my hat became victim of their play."

"Oh, dear," Lily giggled.

"Poor Joe was so embarrassed, but I told him not to worry. I only wish I could afford a new one right now...I don't look forward to wearing that tattered thing for a while...oh—what kind of pie is it?" Stephen touched the steaming crust.

"Pumpkin..."

"Mmm...Can I have a tart?"

"Not until you've kissed the cook."

"Okay."

~~~

"I decided I'll wear my new bonnet today," Lily told Stephen as she finished her hair Sunday morning.

"Fine. I still haven't seen it yet. I'll be out getting the buggy."

As soon as he was gone, Lily dug under the bed and pulled out an object wrapped in brown paper. Unwrapping it, she looked in the mirror and placed the new black Stetson on her head. Then she pulled out her regular straw bonnet. Picking up her handbag, she left the room.

Stephen came through the front door. "Ready, Li..." he stopped in surprise.

"Do you like it?" Lily's eyes sparkled as she turned once to display the hat.

Stephen stood speechless.

"The milliner shop let me return the bonnet; and they gave me full price back. I liked this one the best. And not just because it was half price either. I'd decided on it before the clerk told me the price. So we have four dollars and seventy-five cents left that you can put towards the barn." Lily's satisfaction colored every word.

"I never thought anyone could be so sweet." Stephen pulled the hat off her head and kissed her warmly.

"I'm not sweet." Lily hugged him. "I was just making it right. I could never have worn that bonnet."

"Now that it's over, I'm sort of glad it happened." Stephen released her.

"Why?" Lily asked, following him out the door.

"Well, I think we both learned a lot from our first real quarrel."

"I hope it can be our last," Lily grimaced.

~~~

Lily was at the mercantile attempting to pay for her purchases, when Mrs. Perkins kindly stopped her. "No, that's all right, Lily. These are a gift from Mr. Perkins and I."

"What do you mean?" Lily was totally confused by the older woman's sympathizing tone.

"Mr. Perkins and I want to help as much as we can. Little though it is, we want you to have these and not pay."

"Things aren't that bad, Mrs. Perkins."

"You're so brave, Lily," Mrs. Perkins said as she stifled her tears.

"Thank you, Mrs. Perkins, but if you'll—"

"No, I insist you must count these as a gift," the shopkeeper interjected and continued to remain firm.

"All right—thank you very much." Lily had no comprehension what Mrs. Perkins was talking about. She left the store feeling like a thief and was met by Mrs. Evans.

"Keep faith, Lily, God will be with you," she said, laying a hand on Lily's shoulder before passing on into the store.

Lily thought she glimpsed tears in the eyes of the mayor's wife as she turned. *What is going on?* she wondered.

Passing Mrs. Ellis in the street, she encountered a similar encouragement and began to notice looks of pity and sympathy as she walked down the street. *Something has happened.* Was it her family? Or had something dreadful happened to Stephen?

"Oh, Lily, there you are!"

Lily turned to see Louise and Lauren crossing the street.

"How calm you look in spite of all that he's put you through. I must admit we've had our differences, but I could never be as brave as you," Louise said, shaking her head.

"What do you mean, Louise?" Lily asked.

"You poor dear, so calm amidst what he's done. Well, of course, with all Stephen's deceitful deeds being exposed…" Louise paused. "Well, now everyone knows."

Lauren continued, "I'm so glad Douglas is visiting family in Virginia. I don't know what his anger might bring him to. I couldn't bear to see how he might behave after hearing that Stephen married you after leaving his first wife, even though now his brother-in-law has come to take Stephen back to her."

"What?" Lily couldn't believe her ears. The statement that Stephen had another wife, left Lily totally astonished. Without another word, she ran to the marshal's office, but her father was not there.

"Uncle Mark, what's happened? What is all this about Stephen having been married before? Where's Papa?" she demanded of her father's deputy.

Mark Glenn gently led Lily to a chair and answered her questions. "Your father's in Brockton. Apparently, Bradley Seymour and his sister Adeline—whoever they may be—are there to reclaim Stephen's marriage to Seymour's sister—and the rumor has spread like wild fire through the whole of Four Valley's Township…for both your sakes, I pray it's not true."

Lily swallowed hard. *How can it be? What will I do? Oh, Lord, this has to be a lie!*

Chapter 16

"What room is Bradley Seymour in?" the marshal asked the Brockton Hotel clerk.

"Ahh...room 209—third door on the right."

A well-dressed, thick set man answered the marshal's knock.

"Mr. Seymour?"

"Yes?"

"I'm Marshal Wellington from Oakville. I'd like to talk to you and your sister."

"Come in. My sister is in the adjoining apartment. I'll get her." Seymour stepped aside and let Mr. Wellington enter. "This is my business colleague and close friend, Ernest Howard." He motioned to a narrower man in the room seated in a straight back chair. Mr. Wellington edgily fingered his hat while they waited for Adeline Seymour to take her time in responding to her brother's request. He was repulsed when the woman finally appeared gaudily decked out in a flaunting silk brocade dress.

The marshal plunged into the reason he had come. "Mr. Seymour, am I correct in understanding from rumor that you and your sister are here to see Stephen Bryant?"

"You are."

"May I ask on what account?"

"He's an infidel of the worst kind. Five years ago, he married my sister, Adeline; and not more than two months afterwards, he left her with nothing but a broken heart. Since then, I've hunted him down. Only a few days ago did I find out where he lived."

"Well, you've caused a great stir. I don't think there is a town nearby where you are not talked of." The marshal's eyes noticed the woman's hands nervously feeling the lace edge of a handkerchief as he spoke.

"Yes, I know. I beg pardon for that. We had no intention of causing a stir. But I could not contain my rage when I found out he had not only left my sister, but also betrayed her by marrying another."

Adeline laid a hand on Bradley Seymour's arm. "My brother is not all to blame for letting it be so widely known. I'm afraid I lost all control of myself as well. You can understand the great anguish I feel from his betrayal." Her hands went back to twisting the handkerchief.

"I think you should know that the woman he married is my daughter."

Adeline gasped and shakily brought the handkerchief to her mouth.

Seymour cocked his head in surprise. "So you have a personal interest in this as well…"

"Yes, and I would be obliged if you do as I say. I don't want to see my daughter hurt more than necessary."

"Oh, definitely, I can totally sympathize with her," responded Adeline. "That poor thing—falling for the same trap I did—bewitched by those black eyes."

Mr. Wellington inwardly cringed at her mooning.

"Of course, we'll oblige. But you realize Bryant will deny it. You can't expect any more from a scoundrel like him."

The marshal rose from his chair. "Even so, you'll handle this my way."

"Yes…" Seymour shook Mr. Wellington's hand.

"Good day…Miss Seymour…" the marshal tipped his hat to the lady and left with a heavy heart.

~~~

Lily couldn't do anything but go home after talking to her uncle. She was too distraught to do anything else. When she reached the house, she put her groceries on the kitchen table, went upstairs to their bedroom, collapsed on the bed and wept.

Stephen, meanwhile, was not having a very pleasant day. Progress on William's barn was going much slower than planned. They'd had several setbacks that day.

"If you'll go make that order at the mill, I'll clean up," Will told him.

"Suits me," Stephen replied and rode away.

Charlettedale's main street was busy with people doing their evening errands before supper. Stephen thought he was imagining things when he saw people shying away and avoiding him. Then one elderly woman had the boldness to hiss at him and hit his arm, calling him a beast.

"Ahh, I beg your pardon." Stephen tipped his hat, thinking he had somehow inconvenienced her.

"Something's going on, Thad. Everybody's acting strange. What's up?" Stephen inquired of the mill's clerk.

"What do ya expect when you live like a scoundrel?" Thad Grady's usually candid attitude was replaced with a hostility Stephen had never seen.

"What do you mean? How've I been a scoundrel?"

"Don't act innocent."

"I'm not!"

"Yeah, I know you're not."

"Hey, Thad, no wise cracks. Spit it out! What'd I do?"

"Like I have tell you what you did wrong?"

Stephen felt like punching him. "Okay, never mind then…just take down another two cords of maple for Will, all right?"

"Of all the nerve…I've a mind to knock you senseless. Leaving your first wife after only a month and then coming here and deceiving everyone," Thad spoke as he angrily filled out a register and receipt.

"Where'd you get that lie?" Stephen demanded.

"It's all over town," Thad answered with no less heat. Stephen snatched the receipt from the counter and left. After what Thad had said, he wasn't surprised to meet glares from people he knew as he rode back out of town. *What is this all about? Married before? Who'd tell such a lie?* He looked around at stern faces. *Well, whoever it was has everybody believing it, even in Charlettedale. If Lily ever hears…oh, no!* Stephen spurred Charger into a gallop.

"Lily!" he called, coming through the door. No answer. Upstairs, Lily couldn't bear the thought of facing him.

"Lily!" Stephen looked in the kitchen and saw the groceries on the table. Taking the steps three at a time, he hastened upstairs.

"Lil..." he sat on the edge of the bed and gently laid a hand on her shoulder. Coldly, Lily resisted his touch, sat up and backed away from him.

"Is it true? Were you married before?" she demanded.

"No! Lily, how could you even listen to such things?"

"How could I listen to it? It was right in my face. The groceries are a gift from the Perkins to help out. Mrs. Evans and Mrs. Ellis are telling me to take comfort in God. Louise and Lauren Collins are admiring me for how *brave* I am...and how *calm* I am with the fact that I'm your *second* wife!" She fairly spit out the words. "Where'd it all come from if it's not true?" Lily demanded.

"How should I know? But you've got to believe me—I've never been married to anyone else. I've never loved anyone but you."

Lily sobbed against his shoulder, finally allowing him to hold her.

Not long after, they heard a horse approach. Stephen opened the door to Mr. Wellington.

"I s'pose you've heard what's circulating town..." the marshal said, stepping inside, struggling to remain calm and not rush to judgment. He reminded himself that he had only heard one side of the story.

"I have...you don't believe it, do you?"

"We need to talk, Stephen...where's Lily?"

"She's still upstairs crying. I don't think she believes me."

"Mark told me she came in and wanted the truth, which he had to give her. Well, I went to see Seymour and his sister, they—"

"Wait a minute...start from the beginning. I just barely found out that I was married before."

Sitting down, Mr. Wellington retold the story. At Stephen's response to Adeline's name, he stopped and his face hardened. "You do know her?"

Stephen swallowed hard, the nightmarish part of his life was rearing its head again, only this time with a pretty mask. "Yes— her father was one of my superior officers and I know he did have a son named Bradley, but I never met him. Adeline threw herself at basically every man in the army."

The marshal couldn't catch the stinging accusation before it slipped from his lips. "And you were fool enough to fall for her..."

Stephen's jaw tensed and he ground his teeth against the false charge.

Mr. Wellington shook his head in regret. "I'm sorry, forgive me...I have more reason to believe you than Adeline and Bradley Seymour. What would give them cause to make such an outlandish claim, if it weren't true? The evidence against you is overwhelming…my confidence in your character *and* my daughter's happiness is hinged on this."

"You can just ask Will…"

"I did. He denied it being true because—besides the fact that he knows you—you two were never separated in the war except for when he was hit and spent a month at Luke's—which I hate to say correlates with Seymour's side. I even talked to Luke, but he said that he couldn't know because you two very rarely saw each other. Stephen, I don't want to doubt you—I wish it weren't this way, but I don't know that part of your life. I can only trust you on the basis of the character I've seen since I've known you. I wish I knew what to do with all the wagging tongues until I know the truth."

"How long do you think it'll take to get answers to the telegraphs you sent out?"

"A couple days or so…"

Stephen groaned. The marshal laid a hand on his shoulder not knowing what else to say.

The next morning, Stephen woke up feeling miserable. He had hardly slept. Sitting up, he saw that Lily was already gone. *Lord God, don't let her believe this lie…* he prayed, picking up his Bible. Starting where he had left off the day before in Psalm 119, he began to read. A few verses later, the words seemed to leap from the page as he read the sixty-ninth verse: *The proud have forged a lie against me: but I will keep Thy precepts with my whole heart. Their heart is as fat as grease; but I delight in Thy law...* Stephen exhaled shakily. *God, this is exactly what has happened. Father, get us through this. Show me how to deal with this in a righteous way, so I can honor You and save my reputation...and— more importantly...my marriage, Lord, please don't let Lily believe this terrible lie.*

~~~

"I'm Bradley Seymour, Mrs. Bryant, and this is my sister, Adeline."

Lily's heart wrenched at the sight of the woman she'd seen only once, nearly five years ago. "Yes, we've met once before. Won't you step inside?" Lily braced herself as she motioned for them to sit on the sofa.

Seymour took his seat and began, "I'm sorry things have to be this way. I wish we could just leave you alone, but you see—" Seymour stopped as his sister laid a hand on his arm.

"You see, Mrs. Bryant, or may I call you Lily?"

"Lily's fine."

"Well, Lily," Adeline continued with sympathetic green eyes. "Stephen and I were married in Petersburg almost two months before the end of the war—in fact, I believe our wedding was not long after I visited you, but he made me keep it a secret. Then when General Lee fled to catch up with General Johnston, he swore he'd return for me the very first chance he got. So I let him take all the money we had put together and I stayed with Mother until he came for me, but he never did. He deserted me and left me with nothing but a broken heart." She ended by dabbing at her eyes with a lace-edged kerchief.

"When he left Richmond we lost track of him for some time," Adeline's brother continued for her. "It was just some days ago that we were able to locate him. I was outraged to find that he had not only betrayed my sister, but also deceived you and your family…you see, Mrs. Bryant, Stephen is bound in honor to my sister as her lawful husband."

"You poor thing…how I know what you feel…going through the same thing I have." Adeline shook her head, laying a hand on Lily's.

It took all Lily's willpower not to flee sobbing from the room, and those teary green eyes filled with condescending pity made things worse.

"As an apology for the terrible grief and pain this causes you, I'd like to pay for the nullification of your marriage," Seymour said.

"That's most kind of you, but that won't be necessary." Lily couldn't believe it was her voice she was hearing.

"Ma'am, may I ask where Stephen is? We hope to leave tomorrow—with him," he stated as if everything was planned.

"I—I don't know. He didn't say where he was going when he left this morning." A dreadful thought entered Lily's heart as she fought for control. Did Stephen desert her, too? Subconsciously, Lily fingered her wedding ring, while Stephen's proposal ran through her mind.

"We'll take our leave then. I'm most sorry, Mrs. Bryant. You are sure you don't wish me to pay for the nullification?" Bradley Seymour inquired again.

"I'm quite sure, thank you, though, for your thoughtful generosity and wanting to set things straight for me."

Stoically, Lily bade them goodbye and watched from the window as they rode away. Whatever was she going to do?

~~~

Stephen took a deep breath and knocked on the hotel door bearing the brass numbers 209. It had been two days since he became aware of the rumor. Two long days with almost unbroken silence. Two days living with Lily's silent reserve and distrust.

He couldn't take it any longer. After fasting and constant prayer, Stephen knew how God wanted him to deal with the situation. He would go to the root of the problem and have it out with Seymour and Adeline. What right had she to come claiming him as her husband? He hadn't ever given her a second glance.

The latch clicked and the door opened. Stunned, Stephen staggered back a step. In front of him stood Arnold Setters. Instantly, the pieces fell into place. The words of Brett Whitney's threat four years before echoed through Stephen's mind. "...the day he's gone, I'll be there."

"Didn't expect to see me again, did you?" Arnold seemed pleased at Stephen's reaction.

"You can't get away with this." Stephen regained his composure.

"We can't? We've already got the whole of Brockton, Elton, Oakville and Charlettedale behind us. Even your father-in-law, the marshal. In fact, I don't think your wife even believes you. Brett—or should I say, Brad has paid her a visit with Adeline. They should be back any moment now."

Stephen turned on his heel and left thinking only of how he could keep Lily's trust. But it was too late. Just as he reached the hotel front door, it swung open and he stood face to face with Brett. Immediately, Adeline's histrionics went into play. Grabbing Stephen's arm, she fell on her knees weeping and begging for him to come back to her.

"There you are! Thank you for saving me the trouble of finding you." Brett was pleased with their sudden meeting.

Stephen disdainfully pulled his arm away and stepped back from Adeline. "Sweeney, send for the marshal," he motioned to the desk clerk.

Brett shook his head. "No, don't bother. We'll visit the marshal for ourselves. I think he'll be glad to get this scoundrel out of town." Brett had convinced everyone of his false identity so well that the desk clerk ignored Stephen.

Helping Adeline off the floor, Brett gently told her to go up to her room and prepare to leave after telling Ernest Howard to come downstairs.

"You don't waste time, do you." The inflection in Stephen's voice made the question a statement.

"Not after waiting five years to get a hold of you."

Arnold came down the stairs. "How'd it go, Brad? Didn't expect you back so soon. Got here at the perfect time, though, I see. Poor Adeline's sure shaken up."

"I know, com'on." Brett gave Stephen a rough shove on the shoulder.

Stephen was tense the whole ride, not knowing what Brett or Arnold might do before they reached Oakville.

"What's this, Stephen?" Mr. Wellington stood up when they came into his office.

Before Stephen could open his mouth, Brett spoke. "We'd like to leave tomorrow. So if it's all right with you, we'll—"

"I asked Stephen," the marshal interrupted.

"This is Brett Whitney and Arnold Setters."

"I told you he'd start lying right from the start," Brett scoffed.

"Well, I know someone's lying. And I also know that someone is you…" In a swift motion, the marshal raised the rifle he kept discretely behind his desk. "You see, I checked on your story. Bradley Seymour died in a Ku Klux Klan attack just months after the war ended. Not to mention that a few months ago, someone we knew said you were looking for Stephen. I'm glad to say there is no reason for Stephen's character to be doubted." Mr. Wellington leveled the rifle on Brett. "So I suggest you quietly leave the area—before I find cause to lock you up."

"Didn't want any trouble with the law…" Arnold raised his hands in an indifferent manner and turned to leave. With great reluctance, Brett followed him.

Stephen sighed and slumped in a chair after watching them leave.

"Think they'll be back?" Mr. Wellington asked.

"I know they will. Brett's waited too long for his revenge. He won't walk away. He and Arnold will probably be waiting somewhere for me."

"I was afraid you'd say that. I just wish there were some legal way to arrest them. But I can't—unless they actually attempt to kill you...why don't you ride home and I'll follow you at a distance. We'll see what happens."

It was not until he had turned off the main road that Stephen was jumped on and pulled off his horse. The wind was knocked out of him as he hit the ground with Brett's heavy body on top of his.

"No gun, Brett? Going a little easy, aren't you?" Stephen kept calm.

"No. No gun. I'm going to kill you with my bear hands."

Stephen groaned from the oppressive weight on him and wondered where Mr. Wellington was. A gunshot answered him. *Oh, no! Arnold! Oh, Lord, help!*

"Well, I see Arnold's taken care of your back up." Brett yanked Stephen to his feet. Desperately, Stephen jabbed his elbow into his enemy's ribs. Brett grunted. His hold loosened enough for Stephen to turn and deal a punch, which Brett easily blocked, then returned a hit in Stephen's stomach. Doubling over in agony, Stephen staggered back with the force of the blow. It was impossible for him to out muscle Brett. The man was built like a brick wall.

Stephen's horse, Charger, had shied several yards away and Brett hadn't forgotten the rifle's stock protruding from its holster on Stephen's saddle. Before Stephen could make a move, he was again buffeted with blows. In a final attempt, he forcefully rammed Brett's torso and made a headlong dash for his horse. He just barely had the rifle in his grasp, when Brett's bearlike fist knocked it clattering to the dirt road. But before he could close in on Stephen, Brett's victim dodged his attack and dove for the firearm on the ground.

The moment it took for Brett to regain control cost him his life. Stephen cocked the rifle's lever and squeezed the trigger right on target. Brett Whitney fell heavily to the dirt. Gasping from the burning pain, he stared at Stephen with hate-filled eyes. Then Brett's jaw went slack and his body limp.

Stephen turned and ran back up the road, looking for his father-in-law and Setters. It was a stunning sight he came upon. The marshal was unconscious on the ground and Arnold Setters dead in the ditch.

"Mr. Wellington?" Stephen swallowed hard, rolling his father-in-law over. After a bit of shaking, the marshal regained his faculties.

"Stephen! Are you all right?" were the first words out of his mouth.

"Yeah, what happened?"

"Setters jumped me. I shot him just as he knocked me to the ground. I guess I got knocked out when I hit the road." Mr. Wellington rubbed the back of his head.

"Well, he's dead and so is Brett."

"Thank God you're safe."

"Are you feeling okay?"

"Yeah...my head just hurts." The marshal stood up. "Help me sling their bodies over my horse, then I'll bring them back to town."

"Are you sure you're up to it? You should probably come to the house and rest." Stephen looked skeptical.

"I'm sure. You go to Lily. She needs the truth." The marshal mounted. "You'll never know what a relief it is for me to find that my trust is rightly placed in you, Stephen. For a while...in all honesty...I was scared you'd deceived us."

"I value your trust, Mr. Wellington. I pray I can regain Lily's."

In his earnest desire to get to Lily, Stephen forgot the dull ache of his bruised body. He was so glad when the house came into sight.

"Lily! Lily, I'm home!" he called, eagerly stepping through the door. A horse's nicker answered him from outside. Stephen whirled to see her riding out of the horse shed. "No, Lily!" he forced his stiff legs to move.

His voice brought her head up. Ignoring him, Lily kneed the horse. But Stephen had already clasped the bit in his hand.

"Lily, you're not leaving…" he panted.

"There's no reason for me to stay. You already have a wife waiting for you in Brockton." The anger in her eyes mixed with anguish. "Why, Stephen? Why? How could you hurt me so? How could you do it?" A last "why" came out in a dry sob. Tears didn't help to relieve the intense pain in her heart.

"Lil, I haven't deceived or betrayed you." Stephen lifted her from the saddle. The thought of her leaving terrified him with a fear he'd never realized.

"How can you continue to lie like that?" She struggled against him, but Stephen didn't let go. "It's all out. Seymour *and* Adeline came to see me! How could you have done such a thing?" Angrily, she punched his stomach and the driving pain of Brett's beating was freshly renewed. Doubling over, he let her go with a groan.

"Oh! What happened? Are you all right?" Her anger and hurt were momentarily forgotten.

"I'm just tender there from being ambushed a little bit ago..." Stephen straightened and braced himself against the slowly easing pain. She had to believe him. He couldn't lose her. "It was Brett Whitney. He and Arnold Setters set the whole thing up when they found out where I was. Adeline's real brother is dead."

"What?"

"Brett and Arnold made up the story...ask your father...he has the proof of their lies. I was never married before. There never was anybody else for me."

"Oh, Stephen!" Lily choked on her words in her joyful crying. "I thought I'd lost you!" She clung to him fiercely. "I was so scared!"

Stephen held her for a moment before he pulled her back to see her face. "I've always, only been yours and I always will be. I will never—love any other woman, but you!" His eyes pierced her heart with their earnestness.

"I should've trusted you, Stephen...I'm so sorry..." Lily cried as he kissed her face.

Amid the pain, Stephen held her tightly against him for a long time before he finally released her.

"Tell me all that happened..." Her arms around him, Lily walked with him to the house.

It wasn't long before the marshal had cleared Stephen's name, so that everyone in the district knew the whole truth about what had happened.

Made in the USA
Lexington, KY
03 March 2017